The Stories of
BREECE D'J PANCAKE

※

The Stories of
BREECE D'J PANCAKE

🌾

Foreword by James Alan McPherson

Afterword by John Casey

An Atlantic Monthly Press Book
Little, Brown and Company — Boston–Toronto

Second Printing

Some of these stories have been previously published in
Antaeus, The Atlantic, and *Nightwork.*

"WHEN I'M GONE"
Lyrics and Music by Phil Ochs
© 1966 Barricade Music, Inc. (ASCAP)
All Rights Administered by Almo Music Corp.
All Rights Reserved   International Copyright Secured

"THE WAR IS OVER"
Lyrics and Music by Phil Ochs
© 1968 Barricade Music, Inc. (ASCAP)
All Rights Administered by Almo Music Corp.
All Rights Reserved   International Copyright Secured

"JIM DEAN OF INDIANA"
Lyrics and Music by Phil Ochs
© 1971 Barricade Music, Inc. (ASCAP)
All Rights Administered by Almo Music Corp.
All Rights Reserved   International Copyright Secured

LIBRARY OF CONGRESS CATALOGING IN PUBLICATION DATA
Pancake, Breece D'J, d. 1979
    The Stories of Breece D'J Pancake.
    "An Atlantic Monthly Press book."
    Contents: Trilobites — Hollow — A room forever — [etc.]
    I. Title.
PS3566.A559   813'.54   82-17226
ISBN 0-316-69012-0

ATLANTIC–LITTLE, BROWN BOOKS
ARE PUBLISHED BY
LITTLE, BROWN AND COMPANY
IN ASSOCIATION WITH
THE ATLANTIC MONTHLY PRESS

BP
Designed by Susan Windheim
Published simultaneously in Canada
by Little, Brown & Company (Canada) Limited

PRINTED IN THE UNITED STATES OF AMERICA

CONTENTS

The Stories of
BREECE D'J PANCAKE

FOREWORD

I think you should come over (drive or train, I'll pay your expenses and "put you up") because if you do the preface I feel you should be more familiar with this valley and [my son] Breece's surroundings as well as what you knew of him in Charlottesville.

— Letter from Mrs. Helen Pancake,
February 10, 1981

He never seemed to find a place
With the flatlands and the farmers
So he had to leave one day
He said, To be an Actor.

He played a boy without a home
Torn, with no tomorrow
Reaching out to touch someone
A stranger in the shadows.

Then Marcus heard on the radio
That a movie star was dying.
He turned the treble way down low
So Hortense could go on sleeping.

— "Jim Dean of Indiana,"
Phil Ochs

In late September of 1976, in the autumn of the Bicentennial year, I began my career as a teacher at the University of Virginia. I had been invited to join the writing program there by John Casey, who was then on leave. I had been lent the book-lined office of David Levin, a historian of Colonial American literature, who was also on leave that year. I had been assigned the status of associate professor of English, untenured, at my own request. I had come to Virginia from a Negro college in Baltimore. I had accepted Virginia's offer for professional and personal reasons: I wanted to teach better-motivated students and, on a spiritual level, I wanted to go home.

If I recall correctly, 1976 was a year of extraordinary hope in American politics. James Earl Carter, a southerner, was running for the presidency, and people in all parts of the country, black and white, were looking to that region with a certain optimism. Carter had inspired in a great many people the belief that *this* New South was the long-promised one. And there were many of us who had followed the ancestral imperative, seeking a better life in the North and in the West, who silently hoped that the promises made during the Reconstruction were finally going to be kept. While in the "white" American community Jimmy Carter's candidacy provoked an interest in the nuances of southern speech and in the ingredients of southern cooking, in the "black" American community the visibility of Carter — his speaking in a black Baptist church, his walking the streets of Harlem and Detroit — seemed to symbolize the emergence of a southern *culture*, of which they had long been a part, into the broader American imagination. The emergence of Carter suggested a kind of reconciliation between two peoples shaped by this common culture. His appearance was a signal to refugees from the South — settled somewhat comfortably in other regions — that we were now being encouraged to reoccupy native ground. There were many of us who turned our imaginations toward the ancestral home.

I had left the South at twenty-one, a product of its segregated schools and humanly degrading institutions, and had managed to make a career for myself in the North. Growing up in the South, during those twenty-one years, I had never had a white friend. And although, in later years, I had known many white southerners in the North and in the West, these relationships had been compromised by the subtle fact that a southerner, outside the South, is often viewed as outside his proper context, and is sometimes as much of an outsider as a black American.

Friendships grounded in mutual alienation and self-consciously geared to the perceptions of others are seldom truly tested. They lack an organic relationship to a common landscape, a common or "normal" basis for the evolution of trust and mutual interest. Mutual self-interest — the need of the white southerner to appear "right" in the eyes of sometimes condescending northerners (the South being the traditional scapegoat on all matters racial) and the need of the black southerner for access to somewhat commonly held memories of the South and of southern culture — is the basis for political alliances rather than friendships. To achieve this true friendship, it is necessary for the two southerners to meet on southern soil. And if growing up in the South never presented this opportunity, and if one is still interested in "understanding" that part of oneself that the "other" possesses, it becomes necessary to return to the South. Ironically, while the candidacy of Jimmy Carter represented a political alliance between white and black southerners, the real meaning of the alliance, in 1976 at least, resided in the quality of the personal relationships between these two separate but same peoples on their home ground, in the homeplace. Perhaps this is what I was looking for in the fall of 1976, at Thomas Jefferson's University of Virginia.

I remember two incidents from those first days at Virginia, while I sat in David Levin's book-lined office. An overrefined and affected young man from Texas came in to inquire about my courses, and as I rose from my chair to greet him, he raised his hand in a gesture that affirmed the Old South tradition of noblesse oblige. He said, "Oh, no, no, no, no! You don't have to get up."

The second incident was the sound of a voice, and came several days later. It was in the hall outside my office door and it was saying, "I'm Jimmy Carter and I'm running for President, I'm Jimmy Carter and I'm running for President." The pitch and rhythms of the voice conveyed the necessary messages: the rhythm and intonation were southern, lower-middle-class or lower-class southern, the kind that instantly calls to mind the word *cracker*. Its loudness, in the genteel buzz and hum of Wilson Hall, suggested either extreme arrogance or a certain insecurity. Why the voice repeated Carter's campaign slogan was obvious to anyone: the expectations of the South, especially of the lower-class and middle-class South, were with Carter. He was one of them. His campaign promised to redefine the image of those people whom William Faulkner had found distasteful, those who were replacing a decadent and impotent aristocracy. These were the people whose moral code, beyond a periodically expressed contempt for black Americans, had remained largely undefined in the years since Faulkner.

The bearer of this voice, when he appeared in my doorway, conformed to the herald that had preceded him. He was wiry and tall, just a little over six feet, with very direct, deep-seeing brown eyes. His straw-blond hair lacked softness. In his face was that kind of half-smile/half-grimace that says, "I've seen it all and I still say, 'So what?' " He wore a checkered flannel shirt, faded blue-jeans, and a round brass U.S. Army–issue belt buckle over a slight beer belly. I think he also wore boots. He stood in the doorway, looking into the handsomely appointed office, and said, "Buddy, I want to work with you."

His name, after I had asked it again, was still Breece Pancake.

There was something stiff and military in his bearing. I immediately stereotyped him as of German ancestry (in the South, during its many periods of intolerance, German names have been known to metamorphose into metaphorical Anglo-Saxon ones, Gaspennys and perhaps Pancakes included). He had read some of my work, he said, and wanted to show me some of his. His directness made me wary of him. While I sat at a desk (in academia, a symbol of power), he seemed determined to know me, the person, apart from the desk. In an environment reeking with condescension, he was inviting me to abandon my very small area of protection.

He asked if I drank beer, if I played pinball, if I owned a gun, if I hunted or fished. When these important *cultural* points had been settled, he asked, almost as an afterthought, if he could sign up to do independent study with me. When we had reached agreement, he strolled back out into the hall and resumed shouting, "I'm Jimmy Carter and I'm running for President! I'm Jimmy Carter and I'm running for President!" I recall now that there was also in his voice a certain boastful tone. It matched and complemented that half-smile of his that said, "So what?" Breece Pancake was a West Virginian, that peculiar kind of mountain-bred southerner, or part-southerner, who was just as alienated as I was in the hushed gentility of Wilson Hall.

The University of Virginia, during that time at least, was as fragmented as the nation. There were subtle currents that moved people in certain directions, toward certain constituency groups, and I soon learned that it was predictable that Breece Pancake should come to my office seeking something more than academic instruction. The university, always a state-supported school, had until very recently functioned as a kind of finishing school for the sons of the southern upper class. About a generation before, it had opened its doors to the sons of the middle class. And during the 1960s it had opened them farther to admit women and black students. In an attempt to make the institution a nationally recognized university, an effort was made to attract more students from the affluent suburbs of Washington and from the Northeast. More than this, an extraordinarily ambitious effort was made to upgrade all the departments within the university. Scholars had been recruited from Harvard and Princeton and Stanford and Berkeley and Yale. The institution claimed intellectuals from all parts of the world. The faculty was and remains among the best in the nation.

But these rapid changes, far from modifying the basic identity of the institution, caused a kind of cultural dislocation, a period of stasis in the attempted redefinition of the basic institutional identity. In many respects, it was like a redecoration of the interior of a goldfish bowl. Many of the sons of the southern gentry, seeking the more traditional identity, began attending Vanderbilt, Tulane, Chapel Hill, and Washington and Lee. And while the basic identity of the school remained southern, very few southerners were visible. One result was the erosion of the values that had once given the institution an identity. Another was stratification by class and color considerations. Preppies banded together. So did women. So did the few black students. So did, in their fraternities and clubs, the remnants of the old gentry.

Ironically, the people who seemed most isolated and insecure were the sons and daughters of the southern lower and middle classes. They had come to the place their ancestors must have dreamed about — Charlottesville is to the South what Cambridge is to the rest of the nation — and for various reasons found themselves spiritually far from home. Some of them expressed their frustrations by attacking the traditional scapegoats — black teachers and students. Others began to parody themselves, accentuating and then assuming the stereotyped persona of the hillbilly, in an attempt to achieve a comfortable identity. Still others, the constitutional nonconformists like Breece Pancake, became extremely isolated and sought out the company of other outsiders.

A writer, no matter what the context, is made an outsider by the demands of his vocation, and there was never any doubt in my mind that Breece Pancake was a writer. His style derived in large part from Hemingway, his themes from people and places he had known in West Virginia. His craftsmanship was exact, direct, unsentimental. His favorite comment was "Bull*shit!*" He wasted no words and rewrote ceaselessly for the precise effect he intended to convey. But constitutionally, Breece Pancake was a lonely and melancholy man. And his position at the university — as a Hoyns Fellow, as a teaching assistant, and as a man from a small town in the hills of West Virginia — contributed some to the cynicism and bitterness that was already in him. While his vocation as a writer made him part of a very small group, his middle-class West Virginia origins tended to isolate him from the much more sophisticated and worldly middle-class students from the suburbs of Washington and the Northeast, as well as from the upperclass students of southern background. From him I learned something of the contempt that many upper-class southerners have for the lower- and middle-class southerners, and from him I learned something about the abiding need these people have to be held in the high esteem of their upper-class co-regionalists. While I was offered the opportunity to be invited into certain homes as an affirmation of a certain tradition of noblesse oblige, this option was rarely available to Breece (an upper-class southerner once told me: "I like the blacks. They're a lot like European peasants, and they're *cleaner* than the poor whites"). Yet he was always trying to make friends, on any level available to him. He was in the habit of giving gifts, and once he complained to me that he had been reprimanded by a family for not bringing to them as many fish as he had promised to catch. To make up this deficiency, he purchased with his own money additional fish, but not enough to meet the quota he had promised. When he was teased about this, he commented to me, "They acted as if they wanted me to tug at my forelock."

You may keep the books or anything Breece gave you — he loved to give but never learned to receive. He never felt worthy of a gift — being tough on himself. His code of living was taught to him by his parents — be it Greek, Roman or whatever, it's just plain old honesty. God called him home because he saw too much dishonesty and evil in this world and he couldn't cope.

— Letter from Mrs. Helen Pancake,
February 5, 1981

And I won't be running from the rain, when I'm gone
And I can't even suffer from the pain, when I'm gone
There's nothing I can lose or I can gain, when I'm gone
So I guess I'll have to do it while I'm here.

And I won't be laughing at the lies, when I'm gone
And I can't question how or when or why, when I'm gone
Can't live proud enough to die, when I'm gone
So I guess I'll have to do it while I'm here.

— "When I'm Gone,"
Phil Ochs

Breece Pancake seemed driven to improve himself. His ambition was not primarily literary: he was struggling to define for himself an entire way of life, an all-embracing code of values that would allow him to live outside his home valley in Milton, West Virginia. The kind of books he gave me may suggest the scope of his search: a biography of Jack London, Eugene O'Neill's plays about the sea — works that concern the perceptions of men who looked at nature in the raw. In his mid-twenties Breece joined the Catholic church and became active in church affairs. But I did not understand the focus of his life until I had driven through his home state, along those winding mountain roads, where at every turn one looks down at houses nestled in hollows. In those hollows, near those houses, there are abandoned cars and stoves and refrigerators. Nothing is thrown away by people in that region; some use is found for even the smallest evidence of affluence. And eyes, in that region, are trained to look either up or down: from the hollows up toward the sky or from the encircling hills down into the hollows. Horizontal vision, in that area, is rare. The sky there is circumscribed by insistent hillsides thrusting upward. It is an environment crafted by nature for the dreamer and for the resigned.

Breece once told me about his relationship with radio when he was growing up, about the range of stations available to him. Driving through those mountains, I could imagine the many directions in which his imagination was pulled. Like many West Virginians, he had been lured to Detroit by the nighttime radio stations. But he was also conscious of the many other parts of the country, especially those states that touched the borders of his own region. Once, I asked him how many people there were in the entire state of West Virginia. He estimated about two or three million, with about a hundred thousand people in Huntington, then the state's largest city. It was a casual question, one with no real purpose behind it. But several days later I received in my mailbox a note from him: "Jim, I was wrong, but proportionally correct (Huntington, W.VR. has 46,000 people). To the West, Ohio has approximately 9 million. To the East, Virginia has approx. 4 million. To the South, Kentucky has approximately 3 million. To the North, Pa. has approx. 11 million. West Virginia — 1,800,000 — a million more than Rhode Island. P.S. See you at lunch tomorrow?" It need not be emphasized that he was very self-conscious about the poverty of his state,

11

and about its image in certain books. He told me he did not think much of Harry Caudill's *Night Comes to the Cumberlands*. He thought it presented an inaccurate image of his native ground, and his ambition, as a writer, was to improve on it.

This determination to improve himself dictated that Breece should be a wanderer and an adventurer. He had attended several small colleges in West Virginia, had traveled around the country. He had lived for a while on an Indian reservation in the West. He had taught himself German. He taught for a while at a military academy in Staunton, Virginia, the same one attended by his hero, Phil Ochs. He had great admiration for this songwriter, and encouraged me to listen closely to the lyrics of what he considered Ochs's best song, "Jim Dean of Indiana." Breece took his own writing just as seriously, placing all his hopes on its success. He seemed to be under self-imposed pressures to "make it" as a writer. He told me once: "All I have to sell is my experience. If things get really bad, they'll put you and me in the same ditch. They'll pay *me* a little more, but I'll still be in the ditch." He liked to impress people with tall tales he had made up, and he liked to impress them in self-destructive ways. He would get into fights in lower-class bars on the outskirts of Charlottesville, then return to the city to show off his scars. "These are stories," he would say.

He liked people who exhibited class. He spoke contemptuously of upper-class women with whom he had slept on a first date, but was full of praise for a woman who had allowed him to kiss her on the cheek only after several dates. "She's a lady," he bragged to me. I think that redefining himself in terms of his *idea* of Charlottesville society was very important to Breece, even if that idea had no basis in the reality of the place. Yet there was also an antagonistic strain in him, a contempt for the conformity imposed on people there. We once attended a movie together, and during the intermission, when people crowded together in the small lobby, he felt closed in and shouted, "Move away! Make room! Let people through!" The crowd, mostly students, immediately scattered. Then Breece turned to me and laughed. "They're clones!" he said. "They're *clones!*"

He loved the outdoors — hunting and fishing and hiking in the Blue Ridge Mountains. Several times he took me hiking with him. During these outings he gave me good advice: if ever I felt closed in by the insularity of Charlottesville, I should drive up to the Blue Ridge and walk around, and that would clear my head. He viewed this communion with nature as an absolute necessity, and during those trips into the mountains he seemed to be at peace.

He also loved to play pinball and pool and to drink beer. He was very competitive in these recreations. He almost always outdrank me, and when he was drunk he would be strangely silent. He sat stiff and erect during these times, his eyes focused on my face, his mind and imagination elsewhere. Sometimes he talked about old girlfriends in Milton who had hurt him. He related once his sorrow over the obligation imposed upon him — by a librarian in Milton — to burn and bury hundreds of old books. He liked old things. He talked about hunting in a relative's attic for certain items that once belonged to his father. He recollected letters his father had written, to his mother and to him, in the years before his death.

Breece Pancake drank a great deal, and when he drank his imagination always returned to this same place. Within that private room, I think now, were stored all his old hurts and all his fantasies. When his imagination entered there, he became a melancholy man in great need of contact with other people. But because he was usually silent during these periods, his presence tended often to make other people nervous. "Breece always hangs around," a mutual friend once said to me. He almost never asked for anything, and at the slightest show of someone else's discomfort, Breece would excuse himself and compensate — within a few hours or the next day — with a gift. I don't think there was anyone, in Charlottesville at least, who knew just what, if anything, Breece expected in return. This had the effect of making people feel inadequate and guilty.

Jim, "Bullshit" was one of B's choice sayings — in fact he used to say he wanted his short stories entitled "Bullshit Artist." Love his heart!

— Letter from Mrs. Helen Pancake,
February 5, 1981

The mad director knows that freedom will not make you free,
And what's this got to do with me?
I declare the war is over. It's over. It's over.

— "The War Is Over,"
Phil Ochs

In the winter of 1977 I went to Boston and mentioned the work of several of my students, Breece included, to Phoebe-Lou Adams of *The Atlantic*. She asked to be sent some of his stories. I encouraged Breece to correspond with her, and very soon afterward several of his stories were purchased by the magazine. The day the letter of acceptance and check arrived, Breece came to my office and invited me to dinner. We went to Tiffany's, our favorite seafood restaurant. Far from being pleased by his success, he seemed morose and nervous. He said he had wired flowers to his mother that day but had not yet heard from her. He drank a great deal. After dinner he said that he had a gift for me and that I would have to go home with him in order to claim it.

He lived in a small room on an estate just on the outskirts of Charlottesville. It was more a workroom than a house, and his work in progress was neatly laid out along a square of plywood that served as his desk. He went immediately to a closet and opened it. Inside were guns — rifles, shotguns, handguns — of every possible kind. He selected a twelve-gauge shotgun from one of the racks and gave it to me. He also gave me the bill of sale for it — purchased in West Virginia — and two shells. He then invited me to go squirrel hunting with him. I promised that I would. But since I had never owned a gun or wanted one, I asked a friend who lived on a farm to hold on to it for me.

Several months later, I found another gift from Breece in my campus mailbox. It was a trilobite, a fossil once highly valued by the Indians of Breece's region. One of the stories he had sold *The Atlantic* had "Trilobites" as its title.

There was a mystery about Breece Pancake that I will not claim to have penetrated. This mystery is not racial; it had to do with that small room into which his imagination retreated from time to time. I always thought that the gifts he gave were a way of keeping people away from this very personal area, of focusing their attention on the persona he had created out of the raw materials of his best traits. I have very little evidence, beyond one small incident, to support this conclusion, but that one incident has caused me to believe it all the more.

The incident occurred one night during the summer of 1977. We had been seeing the films of Lina Wertmuller, and that evening *Seven Beauties* was being shown at a local theater. I telephoned Breece to see if he wanted to go. There was no answer. When I called later I let the telephone ring a number of times. Finally, a man answered and asked what I wanted. I asked for Breece. He said I had the wrong number, that Breece did not live there anymore. There was in the tone of his voice the abrupt authority of a policeman. He then held the line for a moment, and in the background I could hear quick and muffled conversation between Breece and several other people. Then the man came on the line again and asked my name and number. He said that Breece would call me back. But then Breece himself took the telephone and asked what it was I wanted. I mentioned the movie. He said he could not see it because he was going to West Virginia that same evening, but that he would get in touch with me when he returned. I left town myself soon after that, and did not see Breece again until early September. That was when he gave me the trilobite, and shortly afterward he made me promise that I would never tell anyone about the night I called him the summer before.

In the early summer of 1978 I left Charlottesville for New Haven, Connecticut. Carter was still President, but my ideas about the South had changed dramatically. I hoped that, with luck, I would never have to return to Charlottesville. I began making plans to resume my old life-style as a refugee from the South. But if life has any definition at all, it is the things that happen to us while we are making plans. In the early fall of that year I found out that I would be a father before spring arrived. Around that same time, a package from Breece, mailed from Charlottesville, arrived at my apartment in New Haven. I did not open it. I knew there would be a gift inside, but I also knew that renewing my connection with Breece would take my memories back to Charlottesville, and I wanted to be completely free of the place. The package from Breece remained unopened until the late evening of April 9, 1979.

On the evening of April 8 I had a dream that included Breece. I was trapped in a room by some menacing and sinister people and they were forcing me to eat things I did not want to eat. Breece was there, but I cannot remember the part he played in the drama. I woke up before dawn to find that my wife's contractions had begun. The rest of the day was spent in the delivery room of the Yale–New Haven Hospital. In the late afternoon I went to the Yale campus and taught a class, which earned me one hundred dollars. Then I walked home, happy with the new direction my life had taken as the hardworking father of Rachel Alice Mc-

Pherson. At my apartment, however, there was a telegram from John Casey, sent from Charlottesville. It informed me that on the previous night Breece Pancake had killed himself.

I called Charlottesville immediately and was told certain facts by Jane Casey, John's wife: Breece had been drinking. He had, for some reason, gone into the home of a family near his little house and had sat there, in the dark, until they returned. When he made a noise, either by getting up or by saying something, they became frightened and thought he was a burglar. Breece ran from the house to his own place. There, for some reason, he took one of his shotguns, put the barrel in his mouth, and blew his head off.

I have never believed this story.

I speculate that Breece had his own reasons for hiding in a neighbor's house. They may have had to do with personal problems, or they may have had to do with emotional needs. Whatever their source, I am sure his reasons were extraordinary ones. As a writer, if I am to believe anything about Breece's "suicide," extract any lesson from it, that lesson has to do with the kind of life he led. I believe that Breece had had a few drinks and found himself locked inside that secret room he carried around with him. I believe that he had scattered so many gifts around Charlottesville, had given signals to so many people, that he felt it would be all right to ask someone to help him during what must have been a very hard night. I believe that he was so inarticulate about his own feelings, so frightened that he would be rejected, that he panicked when the couple came home. Whatever the cause of his desperation, he could not express it from within the persona he had created. How does one say he expects things from people after having cultivated the persona of the Provider? How does one explain the contents of a secret room to people who, though physically close, still remain strangers? How does one reconcile a lifetime of indiscriminate giving with the need for a gesture as simple as a kind word, an instant of basic human understanding? And what if this need is so bathed in bitterness and disappointment that the attempt itself, at a very critical time, seems hopeless except through the written word? In such a situation, a man might look at his typewriter, and then at the rest of the world, and just give up the struggle. Phil Ochs hanged himself. Breece Pancake shot himself. The rest of us, if we are lucky enough to be incapable of imagining such extreme acts of defiance, manage to endure.

Very late in the evening of the day I got the news, I opened the package that Breece had sent me the previous fall. It contained some old photographs of railroad workers, some poetry, and a letter. The first line of the letter told the entire story: "You are under no obligation to answer this." But he had hoped anyway that I would. The pictures were from his family collection, given to him in trust by his Aunt Julia, who was soon to die. He wanted to give them away rather than sell them. The poetry represented an extension of this same impulse. "Also enclosed are some poems you might find interesting — again, I'm not asking for response, just sharing news. I went to Staunton Correctional Institution (the pen) and stumbled onto this guy [an inmate]. Not knowing anything about poetry, I gave [his poems] to [the poet] Greg Orr. . . . He liked them and is doing what he can to help find the proper market thru CODA. Anyway, what was that Latin phrase about the Obligation of Nobility? If it's what I think it means — helping folks — it isn't bad as a duty or a calling. We'd both better get back to work."

Looked at in purely sociological terms, Breece Pancake's work was helping people, giving to people. I think that part of him, the part of West Virginia that borders on Virginia, wanted to affirm those old, aristocratic, eighteenth-century values that no longer had a context, especially in Charlottesville. He was working toward becoming an aristocrat in blue jeans. But he was from the southern lower-middle class, his accent had certain associations, he could find no conventional way to express his own needs, and while he was alive there were many of us who could not understand who or what he was.

Several weeks later, I sent the fossil he had given me, the trilobite, to the girl who had allowed him to kiss her cheek after several dates. She had left Charlottesville, and was then working in New York.

JAMES ALAN MCPHERSON

✲
TRILOBITES

I OPEN the truck's door, step onto the brick side street. I look at Company Hill again, all sort of worn down and round. A long time ago it was real craggy and stood like an island in the Teays River. It took over a million years to make that smooth little hill, and I've looked all over it for trilobites. I think how it has always been there and always will be, at least for as long as it matters. The air is smoky with summertime. A bunch of starlings swim over me. I was born in this country and I have never very much wanted to leave. I remember Pop's dead eyes looking at me. They were real dry, and that took something out of me. I shut the door, head for the café.

I see a concrete patch in the street. It's shaped like Florida, and I recollect what I wrote in Ginny's yearbook: "We will live on mangoes and love." And she up and left without me — two years she's been down there without me. She sends me postcards with alligator wrestlers and flamingos on the front. She never asks me any questions. I feel like a real fool for what I wrote, and go into the café.

The place is empty, and I rest in the cooled air. Tinker Reilly's little sister pours my coffee. She has good hips. They are kind of like Ginny's and they slope in nice curves to her legs. Hips and

21

legs like that climb steps into airplanes. She goes to the counter
end and scoffs down the rest of her sundae. I smile at her, but
she's jailbait. Jailbait and black snakes are two things I won't
touch with a window pole. One time I used an old black snake
for a bullwhip, snapped the sucker's head off, and Pop beat hell
out of me with it. I think how Pop could make me pretty mad
sometimes. I grin.

I think about last night when Ginny called. Her old man drove
her down from the airport in Charleston. She was already bored.
Can we get together? Sure. Maybe do some brew? Sure. Same old
Colly. Same old Ginny. She talked through her beak. I wanted
to tell her Pop had died and Mom was on the warpath to sell the
farm, but Ginny was talking through her beak. It gave me the
creeps.

Just like the cups give me the creeps. I look at the cups hanging
on pegs by the storefront. They're decal-named and covered with
grease and dust. There's four of them, and one is Pop's, but that
isn't what gives me the creeps. The cleanest one is Jim's. It's
clean because he still uses it, but it hangs there with the rest.
Through the window, I can see him crossing the street. His joints
are cemented with arthritis. I think of how long it'll be before I
croak, but Jim is old, and it gives me the creeps to see his cup
hanging up there. I go to the door to help him in.

He says, "Tell the truth, now," and his old paw pinches my
arm.

I say, "Can't do her." I help him to his stool.

I pull this globby rock from my pocket and slap it on the counter
in front of Jim. He turns it with his drawn hand, examines it.
"Gastropod," he says. "Probably Permian. You buy again." I
can't win with him. He knows them all.

"I still can't find a trilobite," I say.

"There are a few," he says. "Not many. Most of the outcrops
around here are too late for them."

The girl brings Jim's coffee in his cup, and we watch her pump back to the kitchen. Good hips.

"You see that?" He jerks his head toward her.

I say, "Moundsville Molasses." I can spot jailbait by a mile.

"Hell, girl's age never stopped your dad and me in Michigan."

"Tell the truth."

"Sure. You got to time it so you nail the first freight out when your pants are up."

I look at the windowsill. It is speckled with the crisp skeletons of flies. "Why'd you and Pop leave Michigan?"

The crinkles around Jim's eyes go slack. He says, "The war," and sips his coffee.

I say, "He never made it back there."

"Me either — always wanted to — there or Germany — just to look around."

"Yeah, he promised to show me where you all buried that silverware and stuff during the war."

He says, "On the Elbe. Probably plowed up by now."

My eye socket reflects in my coffee, steam curls around my face, and I feel a headache coming on. I look up to ask Tinker's sister for an aspirin, but she is giggling in the kitchen.

"That's where he got that wound," Jim says. "Got it on the Elbe. He was out a long time. Cold, Jesus, it was cold. I had him for dead, but he came to. Says, 'I been all over the world'; says, 'China's so pretty, Jim.' "

"Dreaming?"

"I don't know. I quit worrying about that stuff years ago."

Tinker's sister comes up with her coffeepot to make us for a tip. I ask her for an aspirin and see she's got a pimple on her collarbone. I don't remember seeing pictures of China. I watch little sister's hips.

"Trent still wanting your place for that housing project?"

"Sure," I say. "Mom'll probably sell it, too. I can't run the place like Pop did. Cane looks bad as hell." I drain off my cup. I'm tired of talking about the farm. "Going out with Ginny tonight," I say.

"Give her that for me," he says. He takes a poke at my whang. I don't like it when he talks about her like that. He sees I don't like it, and his grin slips. "Found a lot of gas for her old man. One hell of a guy before his wife pulled out."

I wheel on my stool, clap his weak old shoulder. I think of Pop, and try to joke. "You stink so bad the undertaker's following you."

He laughs. "You were the ugliest baby ever born, you know that?"

I grin, and start out the door. I can hear him shout to little sister: "Come on over here, honey, I got a joke for you."

The sky has a film. Its heat burns through the salt on my skin, draws it tight. I start the truck, drive west along the highway built on the dry bed of the Teays. There's wide bottoms, and the hills on either side have yellowy billows the sun can't burn off. I pass an iron sign put up by the WPA: "Surveyed by George Washington, the Teays River Pike." I see fields and cattle where buildings stand, picture them from some long-off time.

I turn off the main road to our house. Clouds make the sunshine blink light and dark in the yard. I look again at the spot of ground where Pop fell. He had lain spread-eagled in the thick grass after a sliver of metal from his old wound passed to his brain. I remember thinking how beaten his face looked with prints in it from the grass.

I reach the high barn and start my tractor, then drive to the knob at the end of our land and stop. I sit there, smoke, look again at the cane. The rows curve tight, but around them is a sort of scar of clay, and the leaves have a purplish blight. I don't wonder about the blight. I know the cane is too far gone to worry about the blight. Far off, somebody chops wood, and the ax-bites echo back to me. The hillsides are baked here and have heat ghosts. Our cattle move to the wind gap, and birds hide in caps of trees where we never cut the timber for pasture. I look at the wrinkly old boundary post. Pop set it when the hobo and soldier days were over. It is a locust-tree post and will be there a long time. A few dead morning glories cling to it.

"I'm just not no good at it," I say. "It just don't do to work your ass off at something you're not no good at."

The chopping stops. I listen to the beat of grasshopper wings, and strain to spot blight on the far side of the bottoms.

I say, "Yessir, Colly, you couldn't grow pole beans in a pile of horseshit."

I squash my cigarette against the floor plate. I don't want a fire. I press the starter, and bump around the fields, then down to the ford of the drying creek, and up the other side. Turkles fall from logs into stagnant pools. I stop my machine. The cane here is just as bad. I rub a sunburn into the back of my neck.

I say, "Shot to hell, Gin. Can't do nothing right."

I lean back, try to forget these fields and flanking hills. A long time before me or these tools, the Teays flowed here. I can almost feel the cold waters and the tickling the trilobites make when they crawl. All the water from the old mountains flowed west. But the land lifted. I have only the bottoms and stone animals I collect. I blink and breathe. My father is a khaki cloud in the cane-brakes, and Ginny is no more to me than the bitter smell in the blackberry briers up on the ridge.

I take up my sack and gaff for a turkle. Some quick chubs flash under the bank. In the moss-dapples, I see rings spread where a turkle ducked under. This sucker is mine. The pool smells like rot, and the sun is a hardish brown.

I wade in. He goes for the roots of a log. I shove around, and feel my gaff twitch. This is a smart turkle, but still a sucker. I bet he could pull liver off a hook for the rest of his days, but he is a sucker for the roots that hold him while I work my gaff. I pull him up, and see he is a snapper. He's got his stubby neck curved around, biting at the gaff. I lay him on the sand, and take out Pop's knife. I step on the shell, and press hard. That fat neck gets skinny quick, and sticks way out. A little blood oozes from the gaff wound into the grit, but when I slice, a puddle forms.

A voice says, "Get a dragon, Colly?"

I shiver a little, and look up. It's only the loansman standing on the creekbank in his tan suit. His face is splotched pink, and the sun is turning his glasses black.

"I crave them now and again," I say. I go on slitting gristle, skinning back the shell.

"Aw, your daddy loved turtle meat," the guy says.

I listen to scratching cane leaves in the late sun. I dump the tripes into the pool, bag the rest, and head up the ford. I say, "What can I do for you?"

This guy starts up: "I saw you from the road — just came down to see about my offer."

"I told you yesterday, Mr. Trent. It ain't mine to sell." I tone it down. I don't want hard feelings. "You got to talk to Mom."

Blood drips from the poke to the dust. It makes dark paste. Trent pockets his hands, looks over the cane. A cloud blocks the sun, and my crop glows greenish in the shade.

"This is about the last real farm left around here," Trent says.

"Blight'll get what the dry left," I say. I shift the sack to my free hand. I see I'm giving in. I'm letting this guy go and push me around.

"How's your mother getting along?" he says. I see no eyes behind his smoky glasses.

26

"Prettv good," I say. "She's wanting to move to Akron." I swing the sack a little toward Ohio, and spray some blood on Trent's pants. "Sorry," I say.

"It'll come out," he says, but I hope not. I grin and watch the turkle's mouth gape on the sand. "Well, why Akron?" he says. "Family there?"

I nod. "Hers " I say. "She'll take you up on the offer." This hot shadow saps me, and my voice is a whisper. I throw the sack to the floor plate, climb up to grind the starter. I feel better in a way I've never known. The hot metal seat burns through my jeans.

"Saw Ginny at the post office," this guy shouts. "She sure is a pretty."

I wave, almost smile, as I gear to lumber up the dirt road. I pass Trent's dusty Lincoln, move away from my bitten cane. It can go now; the stale seed, the drought, the blight — it can go when she signs the papers. I know I will always be to blame, but it can't just be my fault. "What about you?" I say. "Your side hurt all that morning, but you wouldn't see no doctor. Nosir, you had to see that your dumb boy got the crop put proper in the ground." I shut my trap to keep from talking like a fool.

I stop my tractor on the terraced road to the barn and look back across the cane to the creekbed. Yesterday Trent said the bottoms would be filled with dirt. That will put the houses above flood, but it'll raise the flood line. Under all those houses, my turkles will turn to stone. Our Herefords make rusty patches on the hill. I see Pop's grave, and wonder if the new high waters will get over it.

I watch the cattle play. A rain must be coming. A rain is always coming when cattle play. Sometimes they play for snow, but mostly it is rain. After Pop whipped the daylights out of me with that black snake, he hung it on a fence. But it didn't rain. The cattle weren't playing, and it didn't rain, but I kept my mouth shut. The snake was bad enough, I didn't want the belt too.

I look a long time at that hill. My first time with Ginny was in the tree-cap of that hill. I think of how close we could be then, and maybe even now, I don't know. I'd like to go with Ginny, fluff her hair in any other field. But I can see her in the post office. I bet she was sending postcards to some guy in Florida.

I drive on to the barn, stop under the shed. I wipe sweat from my face with my sleeve, and see how the seams have slipped from my shoulders. If I sit rigid, I can fill them again. The turkle is moving in the sack, and it gives me the creeps to hear his shell clinking against the gaff. I take the poke to the spigot to clean the game. Pop always liked turkle in a mulligan. He talked a lot about mulligan and the jungles just an hour before I found him.

I wonder what it will be like when Ginny comes by. I hope she's not talking through her beak. Maybe she'll take me to her house this time. If her momma had been anybody but Pop's cousin, her old man would let me go to her house. Screw him. But I can talk to Ginny. I wonder if she remembers the plans we made for the farm. And we wanted kids. She always nagged about a peacock. I will get her one.

I smile as I dump the sack into the rusty sink, but the barn smell — the hay, the cattle, the gasoline — it reminds me. Me and Pop built this barn. I look at every nail with the same dull pain.

I clean the meat and lay it out on a piece of cloth torn from an old bed sheet. I fold the corners, walk to the house.

The air is hot, but it sort of churns, and the set screens in the kitchen window rattle. From inside, I can hear Mom and Trent talking on the front porch, and I leave the window up. It is the same come-on he gave me yesterday, and I bet Mom is eating it up. She probably thinks about tea parties with her cousins in

Akron. She never listens to what anybody says. She just says all right to anything anybody but me or Pop ever said. She even voted for Hoover before they got married. I throw the turkle meat into a skillet, get a beer. Trent softens her up with me; I prick my ears.

"I would wager on Colly's agreement," he says. I can still hear a hill twang in his voice.

"I told him Sam'd put him on at Goodrich," she says. "They'd teach him a trade."

"And there are a good many young people in Akron. You know he'd be happier." I think how his voice sounds like a damn TV.

"Well, he's awful good to keep me company. Don't go out none since Ginny took off to that college."

"There's a college in Akron," he says, but I shut the window.

I lean against the sink, rub my hands across my face. The smell of turkle has soaked between my fingers. It's the same smell as the pools.

Through the door to the living room, I see the rock case Pop built for me. The white labels show up behind the dark gloss of glass. Ginny helped me find over half of those. If I did study in a college, I could come back and take Jim's place at the gas wells. I like to hold little stones that lived so long ago. But geology doesn't mean lick to me. I can't even find a trilobite.

I stir the meat, listen for noise or talk on the porch, but there is none. I look out. A lightning flash peels shadows from the yard and leaves a dark strip under the cave of the barn. I feel a scum on my skin in the still air. I take my supper to the porch.

I look down the valley to where bison used to graze before the first rails were put down. Now those rails are covered with a highway, and cars rush back and forth in the wind. I watch Trent's car back out, heading east into town. I'm afraid to ask right off if he got what he wanted.

I stick my plate under Mom's nose, but she waves it off. I sit in Pop's old rocker, watch the storm come. Dust devils puff around on the berm, and maple sprigs land in the yard with their white bellies up. Across the road, our windbreak bends, rows of cedars furling every which way at once.

"Coming a big one?" I say.

Mom says nothing and fans herself with the funeral-home fan. The wind layers her hair, but she keeps that cardboard picture of Jesus bobbing like crazy. Her face changes. I know what she thinks. She thinks how she isn't the girl in the picture on the mantel. She isn't standing with Pop's garrison cap cocked on her head.

"I wish you'd of come out while he's here," she says. She stares across the road to the windbreak.

"I heard him yesterday," I say.

"It ain't that at all," she says, and I watch her brow come down a little. "It's like when Jim called us askin' if we wanted some beans an' I had to tell him to leave 'em in the truck at church. I swan how folks talk when men come 'round a widow."

I know Jim talks like a dumb old fart, but it isn't like he'd rape her or anything. I don't want to argue with her. "Well," I say, "who owns this place?"

"We still do. Don't have to sign nothin' till tomorrow."

She quits bobbing Jesus to look at me. She starts up: "You'll like Akron. Law, I bet Marcy's youngest girl'd love to meet you. She's a regular rock hound too. 'Sides, your father always said we'd move there when you got big enough to run the farm."

I know she has to say it. I just keep my mouth shut. The rain comes, ringing the roof tin. I watch the high wind snap branches from the trees. Pale splinters of light shoot down behind the far hills. We are just brushed by this storm.

Ginny's sports car hisses east on the road, honking as it passes, but I know she will be back.

"Just like her momma," Mom says, "racin' the devil for the beer joints."

"She never knew her momma," I say. I set my plate on the floor. I'm glad Ginny thought to honk.

"What if I's to run off with some foreman from the wells?"

"You wouldn't do that, Mom."

"That's right," she says, and watches the cars roll by. "Shot her in Chicago. Shot hisself too."

I look beyond the hills and time. There is red hair clouding the pillow, blood-splattered by the slug. Another body lies rumpled and warm at the bed foot.

"Folks said he done it cause she wouldn't marry him. Found two weddin' bands in his pocket. Feisty little I-taliun."

I see police and reporters in the tiny room. Mumbles spill into the hallway, but nobody really looks at the dead woman's face.

"Well," Mom says, "at least they was still wearin' their clothes."

The rain slows, and for a long time I sit watching the blue chicory swaying beside the road. I think of all the people I know who left these hills. Only Jim and Pop came back to the land, worked it.

"Lookee at the willow-wisps." Mom points to the hills.

The rain trickles, and as it seeps in to cool the ground, a fog rises. The fog curls little ghosts into the branches and gullies. The sun tries to sift through this mist, but is only a tarnished brown splotch in the pinkish sky. Wherever the fog is, the light is a burnished orange.

"Can't recall the name Pop gave it," I say.

The colors shift, trade tones.

"He had some funny names all right. Called a tomcat a 'pussy scat.' "

I think back. "Cornflakes were 'pone-rakes,' and a chicken was a 'sick-un.' "

We laugh.

"Well," she says, "he'll always be a part of us."

The glommy paint on the chair arm packs under my fingernails. I think how she could foul up a free lunch.

Ginny honks again from the main road. I stand up to go in, but I hold the screen, look for something to say.

"I ain't going to live in Akron," I say.

"An' just where you gonna live, Mister?"

"I don't know."

She starts up with her fan again.

"Me and Ginny's going low-riding," I say.

She won't look at me. "Get in early. Mr. Trent don't keep no late hours for no beer drinkers."

The house is quiet, and I can hear her out there sniffling. But what to hell can I do about it? I hurry to wash the smell of turkle from my hands. I shake all over while the water flows down. I talked back. I've never talked back. I'm scared, but I stop shaking. Ginny can't see me shaking. I just walk out to the road without ever looking back to the porch.

I climb in the car, let Ginny kiss my cheek. She looks different. I've never seen these clothes, and she wears too much jewelry.

"You look great," she says. "Haven't changed a bit."

We drive west along the Pike.

"Where we going?"

She says, "Let's park for old times' sake. How's the depot?"

I say, "Sure." I reach back for a can of Falls City. "You let your hair grow."

"You like?"

"Um, yeah."

We drive. I look at the tinged fog, the colors changing hue.

32

She says, "Sort of an eerie evening, huh?" It all comes from her beak.

"Pop always called it a fool's fire or something."

We pull in beside the old depot. It's mostly boarded up. We drink, watch the colors slip to gray dusk in the sky.

"You ever look in your yearbook?" I gulp down the rest of my City.

She goes crazy laughing. "You know," she says, "I don't even know where I put that thing."

I feel way too mean to say anything. I look across the railroad to a field sown in timothy. There are wells there, pumps to suck the ancient gases. The gas burns blue, and I wonder if the ancient sun was blue. The tracks run on till they're a dot in the brown haze. They give off clicks from their switches. Some tankers wait on the spur. Their wheels are rusting to the tracks. I wonder what to hell I ever wanted with trilobites.

"Big night in Rock Camp," I say. I watch Ginny drink. Her skin is so white it glows yellowish, and the last light makes sparks in her red hair.

She says, "Daddy would raise hell. Me this close to the wells."

"You're a big girl now. C'mon, let's walk."

We get out, and she up and grabs my arm. Her fingers feel like ribbons on the veins of my hand.

"How long you in for?" I say.

"Just a week here, then a week with Daddy in New York. I can't wait to get back. It's great."

"You got a guy?"

She looks at me with this funny smile of hers. "Yeah, I got a guy. He's doing plankton research."

Ever since I talked back, I've been afraid, but now I hurt again. We come to the tankers, and she takes hold on a ladder, steps up.

"This right?" She looks funny, all crouched in like she's just nailed a drag on the fly. I laugh.

"Nail the end nearest the engine. If you slip, you get throwed clear. Way you are a drag on the fly'd suck you under. 'Sides, nobody'd ride a tanker."

She steps down but doesn't take my hand. "He taught you everything. What killed him?"

"Little shell fragment. Been in him since the war. Got in his blood . . ." I snap my fingers. I want to talk, but the picture won't become words. I see myself scattered, every cell miles from the others. I pull them back and kneel in the dark grass. I roll the body face-up, and look in the eyes a long time before I shut them. "You never talk about your momma," I say.

She says, "I don't want to," and goes running to an open window in the depot. She peeks in, turns to me. "Can we go in?"

"Why? Nothing in there but old freight scales."

"Because it's spooky and neat and I want to." She runs back, kisses me on the cheek. "I'm bored with this glum look. Smile!"

I give up and walk to the depot. I drag a rotten bench under the broken window and climb in. I take Ginny's hand to help her. A blade of glass slices her forearm. The cut path is shallow, but I take off my T-shirt to wrap it. The blood blots purple on the cloth.

"Hurt?"

"Not really."

I watch a mud dauber land on the glass blade. Its metal-blue wings flick as it walks the edge. It sucks what the glass has scraped from her skin. I hear them working in the walls.

Ginny is at the other window, and she peers through a knothole in the plywood.

I say, "See that light green spot on the second hill?"

"Yeah."

"That's the copper on your-all's roof."

She turns, stares at me.

"I come here lots," I say. I breathe the musty air. I turn away from her and look out the window to Company Hill, but I can feel her stare. Company Hill looks bigger in the dusk, and I think of all the hills around town I've never set foot on. Ginny comes up behind me, and there's a glass-crunch with her steps. The hurt arm goes around me, the tiny spot of blood cold against my back.

"What is it, Colly? Why can't we have any fun?"

"When I was a young punk, I tried to run away from home. I was walking through this meadow on the other side of the Hill, and this shadow passed over me. I honest to god thought it was a pterodactyl. It was a damned airplane. I was so damn mad, I came home." I peel chips of paint from the window frame, wait for her to talk. She leans against me, and I kiss her real deep. Her waist bunches in my hands. The skin of her neck is almost too white in the faded evening. I know she doesn't understand.

I slide her to the floor. Her scent rises to me, and I shove crates aside to make room. I don't wait. She isn't making love, she's getting laid. All right, I think, all right. Get laid. I pull her pants around her ankles, rut her. I think of Tinker's sister. Ginny isn't here. Tinker's sister is under me. A wash of blue light passes over me. I open my eyes to the floor, smell that tang of rain-wet wood. Black snakes. It was the only time he had to whip me.

"Let me go with you," I say. I want to be sorry, but I can't.

"Colly, please . . ." She shoves me back. Her head is rolling in splinters of paint and glass.

I look a long time at the hollow shadows hiding her eyes. She is somebody I met a long time ago. I can't remember her name for a minute, then it comes back to me. I sit against the wall and my spine aches. I listen to the mud daubers building nests, and trace a finger along her throat.

She says, "I want to go. My arm hurts." Her voice comes from someplace deep in her chest.

We climb out. A yellow light burns on the crossties, and the switches click. Far away, I hear a train. She gives me my shirt, and gets in her car. I stand there looking at the blood spots on the cloth. I feel old as hell. When I look up, her taillights are reddish blurs in the fog.

I walk around to the platform, slump on the bench. The evening cools my eyelids. I think of how that one time was the only airplane that ever passed over me.

I picture my father — a young hobo with the Michigan sunset making him squint, the lake behind him. His face is hard from all the days and places he fought to live in, and of a sudden, I know his mistake was coming back here to set that locust-tree post on the knob.

"Ever notice how only blue lightning bugs come out after a rain? Green ones almost never do."

I hear the train coming. She is highballing all right. No stiffs in that blind baggage.

"Well, you know the Teays must of been a big river. Just stand on Company Hill, and look across the bottoms. You'll see."

My skin is heavy with her noise. Her light cuts a wide slice in the fog. No stiff in his right mind could try this one on the fly. She's hell-bent for election.

"Jim said it flowed west by northwest — all the way up to the old Saint Lawrence Drain. Had garfish — ten, maybe twenty foot long. Said they're still in there."

Good old Jim'll probably croak on a lie like that. I watch her beat by. A worn-out tie belches mud with her weight. She's just too fast to jump. Plain and simple.

I get up. I'll spend tonight at home. I've got eyes to shut in Michigan — maybe even Germany or China, I don't know yet. I walk, but I'm not scared. I feel my fear moving away in rings through time for a million years.

✹

HOLLOW

HUNCHED on his knees in the three-foot seam, Buddy was lost in the rhythm of the truck mine's relay; the glitter of coal and sandstone in his cap light, the setting and lifting and pouring. This was nothing like the real mine, no deep tunnels or mantrips, only the setting, lifting, pouring, only the light-flash from caps in the relay. In the pace he daydreamed his father lowering him into the cistern: many summers ago he touched the cool tile walls, felt the moist air from the water below, heard the pulley squeak in the circle of blue above. The bucket tin buckled under his tiny feet, and he began to cry. His father hauled him up. "That's the way we do it," he laughed, carrying Buddy to the house.

But that came before everything: before they moved from the ridge, before the big mine closed, before welfare. Down the relay the men were quiet, and Buddy wondered if they thought of stupid things. From where he squatted he could see the gray grin of light at the mouth, the March wind spraying dust into little clouds. The half-ton cart was full, and the last man in the relay shoved it toward the chute on two-by-four tracks.

"Take a break" came from the opening, and as Buddy set his shovel aside, he saw his cousin Curtis start through the mouth. He was dragging a poplar post behind him as he crawled past the relay toward the face. Buddy watched while Curtis worked the post upright: it was too short, and Curtis hammered wedges in to tighten the fit.

"Got it?" Buddy asked.

"Hell no, but she looks real pretty."

Estep, Buddy's front man, grunted a laugh. "Damn seam's gettin' too deep. Ain't nothin' but coal in this here hole. When we gonna hit gold?"

Buddy felt Estep's cap-light on his face and turned toward it. Estep was grinning, a purple fight cut oozing through the dust and sweat on his cheek.

"Chew?" Estep held out his pouch, and Buddy took three fingers before they leaned against each other, back to back, stretching their legs, working their chews.

"Face is a-gettin' pretty tall;" Estep said. Buddy could feel the voice in his back.

"Same thin's happenin' up Storm Creek," he said, pulling the sagging padding up to his knees.

"An' Johnson's scratch done the same."

"Curt," Buddy shouted, "when'd they make a core sample on this ridge?"

"Hell's bells, I don't know," he said, trying to work in another wedge.

"Musta been sixty years ago," Estep said. "Recollect yer grandaddy shootin' at 'em. Thought they's Philadelfy law'ers."

"Yeah," Buddy laughed, remembering the tales.

From near the opening, where the rest of the relay gathered for air, came a high-pitched laugh, and Buddy's muscles went tight.

"One a-these days I'm gonna wring that Fuller's neck," he said, spitting out the sweet tobacco juice.

"What he said still eatin' at ya?"

"He ain't been worth a shit since he got that car."

"It's Sally, ain't it?"

"Naw, let'er go. Worthless . . ."

The group laughed again, and a voice said, "Ask Buddy."

"Ask 'im what?" Buddy shined his light along the row of dirty faces; only Fuller's was wide with a grin.

"Is Sal goin' back to whorin'?" Fuller smiled.

"Goddamn you," Buddy said, but before he could get up, Estep hooked both his elbows in Buddy's, and Fuller laughed at his struggle. Curtis scrambled back, grabbing Buddy's collar.

"I reckon you all rested 'nough," Curtis shouted, and when they heard coal rattling from the bin to the truck, they picked up their shovels, got into line.

Buddy loosened up, giving in to Curtis and Estep. "Tonight at Tiny's," he shouted at Fuller.

Fuller laughed.

"Shut up," Curtis said. "You and Estep work the face."

Estep let go, and they crawled to the coal face and took up their short-handled spades. The face was already four feet high, and both men could stretch out from their knees, knocking sparkling chunks into the pile, pushing it back for the relay.

"Bet this whole damn ridge is a high seam."

"Make it worth more than ten swats a day."

"By God," Buddy said, and as he dug, wondered if the money would make Sally stay. Remembering Fuller, he hit the face harder, spraying coal splinters into the air.

Estep stopped digging and ran a dirty sleeve across one eye. Buddy was coughing a raspy wheeze, flogging coal to his feet. "Stop killin' snakes — throwin' stuff in my eyes."

Buddy stopped digging. Estep's voice washed over his anger, leaving him small and cold in the glint of the coal face, yet bold and better than Estep or Fuller.

"Sorry, it's just I'm mad," he coughed.

"Get yer chance tonight. C'mon, pace off — one, two . . ."

Together they threw the relay back into rhythm, added speed. The chink of spades and scrape of shovels slipped into their muscles until only the rumble of the returning truck could slow them. The seam grew where it should have faulted, and they hunkered to their feet, digging toward the thin gray line of ceiling.

"Get some picks," Buddy grinned.

"Naw, needs shorin' yet."

Curtis slipped through the relay to the face, his light showing through the dust in up-down streams. When he got down to them, they leaned against the sidewalls to give him room, and he stuck a pocket level to the ceiling, watching as the bubble rose toward the face.

"Knock off till Monday," he said. "We ain't got the timbers fer this here."

As the men crawled out toward the bloom pile, a whisper of laughter seeped back through the mine to the face, and Buddy dropped to his belly to slink outside, unhurried. Even a clam crawl had winded him, and he waited by the chute for Estep and Curtis as the cold air dried his sweat, sealing the dirt to his skin. He could hear, beneath the whining low gears of the coal truck, the barking of a dog down in the hollow. He sat down hard and leaned against the chute.

From the entrance to the hilltop was a wold of twenty yards, the dead stalks of broom sedge rippling in the wind. Buddy figured the overburden of dirt could be moved in a month, the coal harvested in less than a year. He knew Sally would not wait, was not sure he wanted her.

He remembered a time when the price of her makeup and fancy habits would have fed his mother and sisters something besides the mauve bags of commodities the state handed out.

Estep came out, and Buddy offered him a smoke as they watched the truck shimmy under the bin, leveling its load.

"Goddamned cherry picker," Estep grunted toward the driver far down the hill.

"Gonna be lots more cherry — all that goddamned coal." Buddy looked to the western ridges where the sun set a cold strip of fire.

Curtis came up behind them, smiling. "I'm goin' home an' get all drunked up."

"Last time I done that," Estep said, "got me a new baby. Gonna watch ol' Mad Man here so's he don't tear up Tiny's."

"That's where I'll be, by God," Buddy said, as if there might still be something to hold to.

"Just leave 'nough of Fuller to crawl in that doghole on Monday," Curtis said, taking off his cap. Buddy stared at the lines of gray in his hair where the coal dust had not settled.

"I ain't makin' no promises," Buddy said as he started down the path toward the road.

"Pick ya up about eight tonight," Estep yelled, watching Buddy wave his lunch bucket from the trail.

Night rose up from the hollow, and as he came to the dusty access road, Buddy could feel the cold air washing up around him, making him cough. Patches of clouds gathered over the hollow, glowing pink. He turned onto the blacktop road, banging his lunch box against his leg as he walked, and remembered hating Fuller as a boy because Fuller had called him a ridge runner. After twenty years of living in the hollow, he knew why Fuller hated him.

He laughed again at the thought of the coal. He would have a car by fall, and a new trailer — maybe even a double-wide. He tried to think of ways to get Curtis to give up dogholing, and for a moment thought of asking Sally to go into Chelyan with him to look at trailers, but remembered all her talk of leaving.

Through the half-light, he could make out the rotting tipple where his father was crushed only ten days before they shut it down, leaving the miners to scab-work and DPA. The tipple crackled in the cold as the sun's heat left it, and on a pole beside it an unused transformer still hummed. No more coal, the engineers had said, but Buddy had always laughed at engineers — even when he was in an engineer company in the Army. At the foot of the smoldering bone pile where the shale waste had been dumped, Estep's little boy stopped, searching.

"What ya doin' there, Andy?"

"Rocks," the boy said. "They's pitchers on 'em." He handed Buddy a piece of shale.

"Fossils. Ol' dead stuff."

"I'm collectin' 'em."

"What ya wanna save ol' dead stuff for?" he said, handing the shale back.

The boy looked down and shrugged.

"You get on home, hear?" Buddy said, watching as Andy disappeared down the secondary, leaving him to the hum of the transformer. He wondered why the boy looked so old.

As he started back up the road, he could hear the dogs packing up, their howls echoing from the slopes, funneling through the empty tipple. The clouds had thickened, and Buddy felt the first fine drops of a misty rain soak through the dirt on his face. When the trees thinned, he saw his trailer, rust from the bolts already streaking the white paint of last summer. The dogs were just up the road, and he wondered if they could smell Lindy, his bluetick bitch, in the trailer. Sally sat by the window, looking, waiting, but he knew it was not for him.

Lindy smiled at Sally, wagged at the sound of Buddy's footsteps from the bedroom and down the hall. Sally walked away from the door window and set the plates by the stove.

"Estep's stoppin' 'round eight," Buddy said, frowning at the turnips and beans beneath the potlids of supper. "No meat?"

Sally said nothing, but took up her plate and dolloped out her food, leaving the side meat for Buddy. She watched him serve himself, and found herself staring at the freckles of black dust embedded in his face. A dog bark broke her stare, and she went to the table. She could hear them sniffing under the floor.

"They bother hell outa me," she said when Buddy sat.

"Well, she stays in. I don't need no litter of mutts." Buddy mashed fat between his fork prongs, fishing the lean from the mess, and watched Sally eat. "They's gonna be money, Sal."

"Don't start up. They's al's *gonna,* but they ain't never any."

"This time's for sure. Estep an' me, we worked that stuff today. A D-nine dozer an' steam-shovel'd a-fixed us real quick. Curt's got the deed an' all."

"Thought yer folks settled these here ridges."

He remembered standing in the sun at a funeral — he could not say whose, but the scent of Vitalis from his father's hands had turned his stomach, and his new shoes pinched his feet.

"Never had a pot to piss in, neither. Stick 'round, Sal."

With her fork, Sally drew lazy curves in her beansoup, and shook her head. "Naw, I'm tired of livin' on talk."

"This ain't talk. What made ya stay with me this long?"

"Talk."

"Love? Love ain't talk."

"Whore's talk."

His hand flashed across the table, knocking her head askance, and she flushed. She got up slowly, put her plate in the sink, and walked down the hall to the bedroom. Buddy heard her turn on the TV, but the sound died down, leaving only the whimper of the dogs. He watched his plate turn cold, grease crusting the edges.

Getting bourbon for his coffee, he sat his plate on the floor for the bitch, and went to the window. With lamplight shining green in their eyes, the pack circled the trailer, talking, waiting. He turned off the lamp and looked for the thing Sally stared after, but only the light gray sky and near-black ghost of the road touched the hollow.

In the darkness he found his .30-.30 rifle and flashlight, opened the slatted window, and poked them through. Passing over two strong-boned hounds, his beam landed on a ragged spitz, and he fired into the marble-lights, the shot singing through the washes and gullies.

The dogs scattered into the brush beyond the road, leaving the thrashing spitz to die in the yard. Lindy paced the trailer's length to the sound of the whines, but when they stopped, she settled on the couch, her tail flapping each time Buddy moved.

The shot jerked Sally from her half-sleep, but she settled back again, watching the blue TV light play against the rusty flowers of ceiling leaks as the last grains of cocaine soaked into her head. She stretched, felt afloat in an ocean of blue light rippling around her body, and relaxed. She knew she was prettier than the girls in the Thunderball Club, or the girl on the TV, and lots more fun.

"Lotsss," she whispered, over and over.

Buddy's silhouette stood in the doorway. "They won't be back," he said.

"Who?" Sally sat up, letting the sheets slide away from her breasts.

"The dogs."

"Oh, yeah."

"Ya can't make any money at it, Sal. Too much free stuff floatin' 'round."

"Yeah? An' all this money yer makin's gonna keep me here?"

He turned back down the hall.

"Buddy," she said, and heard him stop. "C'mon."

As he shed his shoes, she noticed the slope in his back more than usual, but in turning to her, his chest swelled when he unbuttoned his shirt. From where he stood, the hall light mixed with the TV, flashing her eyes white and pink as she moved in the blanket-wave to make room for him.

He climbed in, his cold hands stroking her waist, and she felt the little tremors in his muscles. She dragged a single finger down his spine to make him shiver.

"When ya leavin?"

"Pretty soon," she said, pulling him closer.

Estep honked his horn again, and Lindy danced by the door, howling.

"I'm comin', dammit," Buddy muttered, buttoning his shirt. The clock on the nightstand glowed ten after eight.

Sally propped her pillow against the headboard and lit another cigarette. As she watched Buddy dress, her jaw tightened, and she rolled ashes from the tip of her cigarette until the fire came to a point. "See ya," she said as he started down the hall.

"Yeah. See ya," he answered, keeping the dog inside as he closed the door.

Outside, the mist mingled with snow, and the spitz lay cold as the water beaded on its fur. Buddy left it to warn the pack, and walked toward the clicking of Estep's engine and the soft clupping of wipers. Before he could open the door, a pain jabbed his lungs, but he held his breath against it, then tried to forget it in the blare of the car's radio.

"Whadya know, Mad Man?" Estep said as Buddy climbed in, coughing.

"Answer me this — Why'd ya reckon Curt wants props for?"

"To shore the damn face, dumbshit."

"An' doghole that goddamn seam, too. He's a ol'-time miner. He loves doin' all that ol'-time shit."

"Whadya drivin' at?"

"How many ya reckon'd walk out if I's to dump the water Monday?"

"Buddy, don't go callin' strike. I got family."

"C'mon — how many ya reckon?"

"Most," Estep said. "Maybe not Fuller."

Buddy nodded. "I'd say so, too."

"Yer talkin' weird. Curt's kin — ya can't go callin' strike on yer kin."

"I like Curt fine," Buddy coughed. "But I'm tellin' ya they's a easy way to run that coal."

"Won't work, Buddy. Operation like that'd put ever'body outa work. 'Sides, land ain't good fer nothin' after ya strip."

"That land," he gagged, "that land ain't no good noway, and we could so use work. We'd use ever'body in our hole. An' Storm Creek. An' that piddlin' of Johnson's. Fair an' equal. Know how much that'd be?"

"Can't be much with all the fellars in the line."

"Try on fifty thou. Does it fit?" He slapped Estep's arm. "Well, does it?"

"Where'd we get the machines?"

"Borrow on the coal. Curt's got the deed — just needs some new thinkin' put in his head's all. You with me?"

"I reckon."

They rode, watching the snow curve in toward the lights, melting on the windshield before the wiper struck it. Through the trees, Buddy could see the string of yellow light bulbs above the door and windows of Tiny's.

"Johnson found out who's stealin' his coal," Estep said, letting the car slow up. "Old Man Cox."

"How's he know for sure?"

"Drikked a chunk an' put in a four-ten shell. Sealed 'er over with dust an' glue."

"Jesus H. Christ."

"Aw, didn't hurt 'im none. Just scared 'im," Estep said, guiding the car between chugholes in the parking lot.

Buddy opened his door. "Man alive, that's bad," he mumbled.

Inside Tiny's, Buddy nodded and waved to friends through the smoke and laughter, but he did not see Fuller. He asked Tiny, but the one-eared man only shrugged, setting up two beers as

Buddy paid. He walked to the pool table, placed his quarter beside four others, and returned to lean against the bar with Estep.

"Slop," Buddy yelled to one of Johnson's shots.

"Slop you too," Johnson smiled. "Them quarters go fast."

Fuller came in, walked to the bar, and shook his head when Tiny came up.

" 'Bout time ya got here," Buddy said.

"Sal's out yonder. Wants to talk to ya."

"Whadya got? Carload of goons?"

"See fer yerself." Fuller waved toward the window. Sally sat with Lindy in the front seat of Fuller's car. Buddy followed Fuller outside motioning for Sally to roll down the window, but she opened the door, letting Lindy out.

"You baby-set for a while," she said.

Fuller laughed as he started the car.

Buddy bent to collar Lindy, but she stayed by him. Straightening himself, Buddy looked after the car and saw his TV bobbing in the back seat.

"C'mon," Estep said from behind him. "Let's get drunked up an' shoot pool."

"Yer on," Buddy said, leading the dog into the bar.

Buddy lay on the trailer's carpet, a little ball of rayon batting against his nostril as he breathed, and tried to remember how he got there, but Sally's smile in his mind jumbled him. He remembered being driven back by Estep, falling down in the parking lot, and hitting Fred Johnson, but he did not know why.

He stood up, shook himself, and leaned down the hall to the bathroom. The blood flow from his head and the shock of the light turned the room purple for a moment, and he ran water from the shower on his head to clear the veil. Looking into the mirror, he saw the imprints of the carpet pattern on his cheek, the poison hanging beneath his eyes. He wanted to throw up but could not.

"Ol' dead stuff," he muttered, and heaved dryly.

Atop the commode sat a half-finished bourbon Coke, and he tossed it down, waiting for it to settle or come up again. Leaning against the wall, he remembered the dog, called to her, but she did not come. He looked at his watch: it was five-thirty.

He went into the living room and opened the door — the wet snow was collecting in patches. He called Lindy, and she came to him from behind the trailer, a hound close behind her. He shut the door between the dogs and sat on the couch. Lindy hopped up beside him. "Poor old girl," he said, patting her wet side. "Yer in fer the works now." His knuckles were split, and blood flaked from his fingers, but he could not feel any burning.

"Sal's gone, yes, she is. Yes, she is. Couple of months, an' we'll show her, yes we will." He saw himself in Charleston, in the Club, then taking Sally home in his new car . . .

"Hungry, ol' girl? C'mon, I'll fix ya up."

In the kitchen, he looked for fresh meat to treat her, and finding none, opened a can of sardines. Watching her lap them up, he poured himself a bourbon, and feeling better, leaned against the counter. Sally's plate lay skinned with beansoup in the sink, and for a moment he missed her. He laughed to himself: he would show her.

Lindy walked under the table and coughed up her sardines.

"Don't blame ya a damn bit," he said, but in the roil of sardines and saliva, he saw himself cleaning it up, knew the smell would always be there. There was no reason he should have to clean up, no reason he could not have meat, or anything he wanted. He took up his rifle, leaning where he had left it, and Lindy barked around his heels. "No," he shouted, hanging her by the collar from his forefinger until he could shut the door.

Outside the snow fell harder and in thick, wet lumps, making patterns in the darkness. The climb up the hill to the ridge behind the trailer stirred his lungs to bleeding, and he stopped to spit and breathe. Rested, he walked again in a quiet rhythm with the rustle of snow on the dead leaves.

In the brush by the trail, a bobcat crouched, waiting for the man to clump by, 'its muscles tight in the snow and mist. Claws unsheathed, it moved only slightly with the sounds of his steps until he was far up the trail, out of sight and hearing. The cat moved down the trail, stopping only to sniff the blood-spit the man had left behind.

By the time Buddy crested the ridge, he could feel the pain of trailer heat leave his head, and he stopped short of the salt blocks he had laid out last fall. He held in a breath to slow the wheezing, and when it stopped, sat on his old stump, watching the first mild light of the sky glow brown. He loaded his gun and watched a low trail in the brush, a trail he saw through outlines of snow in the ghost light. From the hollow, dog yelps carried to the ridge. The trail was empty.

Behind him, something rattled in the leaves, and he turned his head slowly, hearing the bones in his neck click. In the brown light he made out the rotted ribs of an old log barn he had played in before they sold the land, moved to the hollow. Something scurried past it, ran away from him, and up the ridge. From the baying of the dogs below, he was sure it was a fox.

Between the clouds and the hills hung the sun, moving fast enough to track, making the snow glisten on the branches. When he looked away from the sun, his eyes were drawn to the cool shadow of a deer standing against the yellow ribbon of sunlight.

He moved slowly, lifting the gun to his face, aiming into the shadow, and before the noise splintered into the hollow, he saw a flash of movement. He ran to the place where the deer had stood, but there was no blood. He tracked the animal only ten yards to where it had fallen. It was a doe with a pink lip of wound near her shoulder, but no blood.

Working quickly, he split her hind tendons, threaded them with a stringer, and hoisted her from a low limb. He cut across the throat, and blood dripped into the snow, but as he ran the knife up the belly, something inside the carcass jolted, moved against the knife point. He kept cutting, and when the guts sagged out, a squirming lump fell at his feet.

He kicked the unborn fawn aside, disconnected the doe's guts, sliced off the hindquarters, and let the rest of the carcass fall for the scavengers to find. He laid three small slices of liver aside in the snow to cool.

Warm doe blood burned his split knuckles, and he washed them with snow, remembering why he had hit Fred Johnson — for spiking Old Man Cox's coal. He began to laugh. He could see Old Man Cox screaming his head off. "Shit," he laughed, shaking his head.

He bit off a piece of the cool raw liver, and as it juiced between his teeth, watched the final throes of the fawn in the steamy snow. He could not wait to dump the water at the mine tomorrow, and laughed as he imagined the look on Curtis's face. "Strike," he muttered over and over.

On a knoll in the ridge, run there by the dogs, the bobcat watched, waiting for the man to leave.

A ROOM FOREVER

BECAUSE of New Year's I get the big room, eight-dollar room. But it seems smaller than before; and sitting by the window, looking out on the rain and town, I know the waiting eats at me again. I should never show up in these little river towns until my tug puts in — but I always come early, wait, watch people on the street. Out there vapor lamps flicker violet, bounce their light up from the pavement, twist everything's color. A few people walk along in the drizzle, but they don't stop to look into cheap-shop windows.

Aways past the streets I see the river in patches between buildings, and the black joints of river are frosted by this foggy rain. But on the river it's always the same. Tomorrow starts another month on the river, then a month on land — only the tales we tell will change, wrap around other times and other names. But there will be the same crew on the *Delmar*, the same duty for eighteen hours a day, and pretty soon there won't be tales. For now, I wait, watch the wind whip rain onto the panes and blur the glass.

I plug in the hot plate for coffee, look through the paper for something to do, but there is no wrestling or boxing for tonight, and even the bowling alley is closed for New Year's. I could maybe go down to a bar on First Avenue, sort of tie one on, but not if I have to watch barge rats and walk the wet steel edges tomorrow. Better to buy a pint and whiskey myself into an early sack, better not to think about going out.

I down my coffee too soon, burn my mouth. Nothing ever goes just the way it should. I figure that is my bitch with New Year's — it's a start all right — only I think back on parties we had in the Navy, and how we pulled out the stops the year we got to be short-timers, and it leaves me feeling lousy to sit here thinking about parties and work and the baby year and the old worn-out year. I want to haul my ass out of here — I have been inside too long.

I get my jacket and watch cap, then stand outside my door and light a cigarette. The hall and stairwell are all lit up to keep away the whores and stumblebums. The door across the hall opens and the drag queen peeks out, winks at me: "Happy New Year." He closes his door quietly, and I cut loose, kick the door, smudge the paint with my gum soles. I hear him in there laughing at me, laughing because I am alone. All the way down the stairs I can hear his laugh. He is right: I need a woman — not just a lousy chip — I need the laying quiet after that a chip never heard of. When I come to the lobby full of fat women and old men, I think how this is all the home I have. Maybe I have bought this room forever — I just might not need another flop after tonight.

I stand under the marquee, smoke, look back into the lobby at the old cruds. I think how all my fosters were old and most of them dead by now. Maybe it's better they are dead or I might go back and visit them and cramp their style. There wouldn't be any welfare check tied to me now, and I am too big to be whipped.

I toss my cigarette, watch it bob down the gutter-wash and through the grate. It will probably be in the Mississippi before the *Delmar*. Moping around these towns for nine months has made me screwy; walking barges and securing catheads in high water has finally got me down here with the rest of the cruds. Now my mouth hurts from the coffee burn, and I don't even feel like getting soused. I walk down the street, watch people as they pass, and think how even the chippies in their long vinyl coats walk like they have someplace to be. I think I am getting pretty low if these old sows are starting to look good.

I walk until I see a stumblebum cut into a passage between two buildings. He has got his heat in him and he is squared away. I stop to watch this jake-legger try to spread out his papers for a bed, but the breeze through the passage keeps stirring his papers around. It's funny to watch this scum chase papers, his old pins about ready to fold under him. The missions won't let him in because he is full of heat, so this jake-legger has to chase his papers tonight. Pretty soon all that exercise will make him puke up his heat, and I stand and grin and wait for this to happen, but my grin slips when I see her standing in that doorway.

She is just a girl — fourteen, fifteen — but she stares at me like she knows what I'm thinking, what I'm waiting to see with this old bum, and she keeps looking at me like she is the Wrath of God or something. My eyes hurt to watch her from the side while I keep my face on the stumblebum, but I watch just the same. I can tell right off she is not a chippy. Her front is more like a kid who had a home once — jeans, a real raincoat, a plastic scarf on her head. And she is way too young for this town — the law won't put up with fresh chicken in this place. I think she has probably run off, and that type is hard to figure out. I walk past her, pay no attention, then duck into a doughnut shop.

Prince Albert sits at the counter talking to himself, running rusty fingers through his hair and beard. His skin is yellowish because he cauterized his brain with a forty-volt system aboard the *Cramer*. I hear he was a good wireman, but now he is just a gov't suck, and he is dirty and smells like any wino on the street.

I eat my sinker, sip coffee and look out the window. Traffic thickens, the parties are building up. That girl walks by, looks in the storefront at me like she knows exactly when I'm going to fall between two barges in a lurch. It gives me the creeps and I leave my coffee, go for some whiskey and a nap, but when I get outside, she is far down the street, going toward the shanty bars on First Avenue. The rain blows up a howl, whipping sheets of water along the sidewalks. I follow her until she gets into another doorway. My watch cap is soaked, and water starts running down my face and neck, but I go to her doorway, stand in the rain looking at her.

She says, "You want to buy me?"

I stand there for a long time trying to figure if it's a coneroo. "You got a room?" I say.

She shakes her head, looks across the street, then up and down it.

"We'll use mine, but I want some booze."

"All right, I know a place that sells it," she says.

"I know a better place." I am wise to that trick. I am not about to let her pimp roll me. But it bugs me — I can't figure what kind of pimp wouldn't keep a room. If she is working alone she won't last two days between the cops and the pimps.

We go on down the street to a state store. It is good to have somebody to go along with, but she looks too serious, like all she thinks about is the business end of this. I buy a pint of Jack Daniel's, try to joke. "Jack and me go way back," I say, but she acts like she can't hear me.

When we walk into the lobby of the hotel, two old men stop talking to look at us. I think how they must have the hots for her, envy me, and I am glad these cruds are paying attention. At my door, I take my time unlocking, and hope the queen peeks out, but he is off getting buggered. We go in, and I get us a towel to dry off, make coffee for the whiskey.

"It's nice here," she says.

"Yeah. They spray regular."

For the first time she smiles, and I think how she ought to be off playing jacks or something.

"I'm not much good at this," she says. "The first guys hurt me pretty bad, so I'm always sort of scared."

"That's because you ain't cut out for it."

"No, it's just I need a place. I got to stop moving around, you know?"

"Yeah." In the window I see our ghosts against the black gloss of glass. She puts her arm around me, and I think how we maybe never left the business end.

"Why'd you come to me?" she says.

"You looked at me funny — like you seen something awful was going to happen to me."

She laughs. "Well, I didn't. I was sizing you."

"Yeah. I'm just jittery tonight. I'm second mate on a tug. It's kind of dangerous."

"What's a second mate do?"

"Everything the captain or first mate won't do. It ain't much of a life."

"Then why don't you just quit?"

"Some things are worse. Quits ain't the answer."

"Maybe not."

Her hand on my neck teases me into smiling about her, liking her. "Why don't you quit trying to be a chippy? You ain't got the stuff. You're better than that."

"It's nice you think so," she says.

I look at her, think what she could be if she had a break or two. But she won't get them here. Nobody here gets a break. I could tell her about my fosters or the ladies in the welfare offices, and the way they looked at me when they put me on a bus for another town, but it wouldn't make any sense to her. I turn off the light and we undress, get into bed.

57

The darkness is the best thing. There is no face, no talk, just warm skin, something close and kind, something to be lost in. But when I take her, I know what I've got — a little girl's body that won't move from wear or pleasure, a kid playing whore, and I feel ugly with her, because of her. I force myself on her like the rest. I know I am hurting her, but she will never get any breaks. She whimpers and my body arches in spasms, then after, she curls in a ball away from me, and I touch her. She is numb.

I say, "You could stay here this month. I mean if you wanted to, I could pay up the rent and you could get a real job and pay me back."

She just lays there.

"Maybe you could get work uptown at Sears or Penney's."

"Why don't you just shut-the-fuck-up." She climbs out of bed. "Just pay me off, okay?"

I get up, find my pants, peel off twenty and give it to her. She doesn't look at the bill, but grabs her coat, runs out the door.

I sit on the bed, light a cigarette, and my skin crawls to think what could happen to that girl; then I tell myself it was just a waste of time and money. I think back to high school when I was courting Jane. Her parents left us alone in the living room, but her poodle kept screwing at my leg. There we were trying to talk and her dog just kept humping my leg. I think I'd like to get a car and go back looking for that dog, but it is always like that — a waste of time and money.

I snipe my cigarette, lay back on the bed with the light on, and think about Prince Albert with sinker crumbs in his beard, coffee stains on his shirt. I think how there must be ten of his kind in every town down to the delta, and how the odds on ending up that way must be pretty low. Something goes screwy and they grab the wrong wire, make a stupid move on the locks. But if nothing goes wrong, then they are on for a month, off for a month, and if they are lucky they can live that way the rest of their days.

58

I dress and go out again. It is still raining and the cold pavement shines with new ice. Between the buildings the bums are sleeping in the trash they have piled up, and I think about some nut in California who cut winos' throats, but I can't see the percentage. The stumblebums are like Prince Albert, they ran out of luck, hit the skids.

I turn onto First Avenue, walk slowly by the row of crowded taverns, look in the windows at all the lucky people getting partied up for New Year's. Then I see her sitting at a table near the back door. I go in, take a stool at the bar, order a whiskey, neat. The smoke cloud is heavy, but I see her reflection in the mirror behind the bar. From the way her mouth is hanging limp I see she is pretty drunk. I don't guess she knows she can't drink her way out of this.

I look around. All these people have come down from their flops because there are no parties for them to go to. They are strangers who play a little pool or pinball, drink a little booze. All year they grit their teeth — they pump gas and wait tables and screw chippies and bait queers, and they don't like any of it, but they know they are lucky to get it.

I look for her in the mirror but she is gone. I would have seen her going out the front, so I head for the back door to look for her. She is sitting against a building in the rain, passed out cold. When I shake her, I see that she has cut both wrists down to the leaders, but the cold rain has clotted the blood so that only a little oozes out when I move her. I go back inside.

"There's some girl out back tried to kill herself."

Four guys at the bar run out to her, carry her inside. The bartender grabs the phone. He says to me, "Do you know her?"

I say, "No. I just went for some air." I go on out the door.

The bartender yells, "Hey, buddy, the cops'll want to see you; hey, buddy . . ."

I walk along the avenue thinking how shit always sinks, and

how all these towns dump their shit for the river to push it down to the delta. Then I think about that girl sitting in the alley, sitting in her own slough, and I shake my head. I have not gotten that low.

I stop in front of the bus station, look in on the waiting people, and think about all the places they are going. But I know they can't run away from it or drink their way out of it or die to get rid of it. It's always there, you just look at somebody and they give you a look like the Wrath of God. I turn toward the docks, walk down to see if the *Delmar* maybe put in early.

✹

FOX HUNTERS

THE passing of an autumn night left no mark on the patch-
work blacktop of the secondary road that led to Parkins. A
gray ooze of light began to crest the eastern hills above the hollow
and sift a blue haze through the black bowels of linking oak branches.
A small wind shivered, and sycamore leaves chattered across the
pavement but were stopped by the fighting-green orchard grass
on the berm.

The opossum lay quietly by the roadside. She had found no
dead farm animals in which to build her winter den; not even a
fine empty hole. She packed her young across the road and into
the leaves where the leathery carcass of another opossum lay.
She did not pause for sniffing or sentiment.

Metalclick. She stopped. Fire. She hunkered in tight fear against
the ground, her young clutching closer to her fur. Soft, rhythm-
less clumpings excited her blood, and she sank lower. With day
and danger advancing, fear was blushing in her as she backed cau-
tiously into higher brush. From her hiding, she watched a giant
enemy scuffling on the blacktop, and a red glow bouncing brightly
in the remnant of her night.

Bo felt this to be the royal time of his day — these sparse, solitary
moments when the rest of the world was either going to bed or not
up yet. He was alone, knew the power in singularity, yet was
afraid of it. Insecurity crawfished through his blood, leaving

him powerless again. Soon he began a conversation to make the light seem closer to the road.

"Coffee, Bo," he said to himself.

"Yeah, and Lucy, toosie," he answered.

"And putin*tane*."

"Yeah," and he quickened his pace, imitating a train.

"*Pu*tintane, *pu*tintane, pu*n*tane, p'*tane*, woooo."

The opossum crouched lower. Her unready, yet born, offspring clung to her belly, nudging to nurse.

His pace lagged back. Maybe Lucy was a whore, but how in the hell would he know? He liked the way she leaned over the grill, showing slip and garters, and knowing it, still, acting vaguely embarrassed. He liked the way she would cock her head to the right, nod solemnly, brows pursed in wrinkled thought, while he talked about cities he had seen on TV. Or about his dad, who sucked so much mine gas, they had to bury him closed-coffin because he was blue as jeans. Bo would live out a reckless verbal future with Lucy. She listened. Occasionally she advised. Once he was going to run off to New York and get educated. Just chuck it all, leave his mother, and get educated in New York. He had felt silly and ashamed when Lucy said to finish high school first. Times like that, he left the dinette convinced Lucy was a whore.

From up the road, he could hear the rumble of Enoch's truck. Instinctively, he jumped over the embankment, slipped into the brush, and squatted. A hiss came from within the brush. Bo turned to see a gray-white form in the fog beside him. It looked like a giant rat with eyebrows. They stared, neither wanting any part of the other — the opossum frozen between acting dead or running, Bo crouching lower as the headlights neared. It was only two more miles to Parkins, but if Enoch saw him he would stop; then Bo would be "crazy boy" at the garage for another week because he would rather walk than ride with his boss.

The truck clattered by, its pink wrecker rig swinging, erratic pendulum of pulley, hook, and cable.

Bo unzipped his pants and pissed with frozen opossum eyes looking on. Steam rose from the puddle, and he shuddered as it drifted to intermingle with the blue mist. He began wading leaves up the embankment.

As he trampled the orchard grass at the berm, another truck could be heard up the road, and he fought the urge to slide back down the slope. He could not explain why he wanted to walk, nor was he certain he wanted to walk anymore. He stepped onto the pavement feeling tired and moved a few paces until headlights flooded his path, showing up the highway steam and making the road give birth to little ghosts beneath his feet.

The truck thundered up behind, then let three high-pitched whines pierce the road spirits of the morning. Bo waited for the truck to stop. When it did, a voice called: "Git in er git ober."

Bo whirled to look at the driver but found his eyes drawn to the white oblivion of the headlights. "Bill?" was all he was able to say as his eyes made red and purple dots appear in the lights.

"Hell yes. You blind?"

Bo looked to the gray hills to drag his attention from the lights, and slowly remembered every detail of Lucy's body as it disintegrated into his brain. Breast hair. Jesus Christ, how long had he stood in that light like a fool? Bill would tell everybody that Bo Holly was out of his goddamned mind. He groped to the truck, rubbing the red dots into his eyes with his hands.

"Git in," said Bill, while his eyes explored Bo with the same scrutiny he had once used to search a two-headed calf for stitches around either head. Bo gave a little sigh as he climbed into the truck's cab, and Bill pounced with the question: "You sick?"

"Just not awake yet," Bo lied. He felt professional about lying, and once started, would not stop. "Momma overslept. Got me up and out without coffee and half dressed. Said I was late to work. What time is it, Bill?" Questions and complex sentences, Bo had learned, were the great shield of liars. Bill studied his wristwatch, then sneered at the sky as if *The Black Draught Almanac* had been two days off on its sunrise schedule.

"Ten abter seben," he growled, pounding his hand against the wheel.

"Shit," Bo yelled, watching Bill jump a little. "But Enoch probably ain't there yet. He's always late. Didn't come in last Saturday till eleven."

"Ain't none of *my* biz-whacks," Bill snapped. "By god, I mind my own biz-whacks." But Bo knew Bill would remember this as a gossip gift to a bored wife.

"I's talkin' to Larry up to the Union Hall," said Bill, experimenting shamefully, "an' he says yer faberite song's that damn 'Rockin' Riber.' "

" 'Rollin' on the River'?" Questions don't give offense, he thought, besides, the song's "Proud Mary."

"Stupid song, Bo. You oughta know better."

Bo said nothing.

"Son' like that's ber a riber town. We ain't got no riber in Parkins."

"Got the Elk in Upshur. Watch this pothole." The truck jolted twice. "Guess it's eat up the whole road." Bill had to think to remember where he had left off. Elk?

"The Elk ain't nothin' to sing about," he cackled. "Now, Merle Haggard, he can tell ya . . ."

"S'matter, Bill, ain't you proud to be a West Virginian?"

"Sure, goddammit, but a song like that's ber eberbody eberwhere. You just don't listen to no good stuff, do ya?"

Bo settled back in his seat, stuck his feet under the heater, and once they were warm enough to feel cold, decided why he liked Lucy: she was a genuine person.

In the silence, the opossum thawed, and was carefully slipping up the bank, sniffing after the danger once so close. It paused in the sycamore leaves and wet orchard grass, then scuttered across the blacktop and back into the woods the way it had come. It was almost morning.

When Bill's truck topped the final grade into Parkins, the sun had already begun to ricochet from the western slopes, and the eastern hills cast a gray shadow over the town. From that grade, Bo could see who was up and who wasn't by the positions of yellow squares of light on the houses. Lucy was in the kitchen of her boardinghouse, her tenants in the bathrooms. The two Duncan sisters, who did nothing, rose early to get on with it. They gossiped about their neighbors, mostly about Lucy. She ignored them. Bo thought she liked to be talked about.

Brownie Ross was opening his general store near the railroad; turning on lights, raising blinds, shoveling coal into the stove. Bo wondered why Brownie opened so early — Enoch, too. Brownie never sold anything bigger than a quarter-sack of nails before noon, and if your car broke down, you'd have to walk to Parkins for a phone.

Bill worked for the railroad — station manager — and Lucy boarded the few men the reopened mine demanded, so both had to be up and going by six. Enoch opened early because Brownie did, and Brownie was just old. Mornings changed very little in Parkins.

"Just let me off at the boardin'house, Bill. I want a cuppa coffee."

"Ain't none of *my* biz-whacks," Bill snapped as the truck stopped beside the laughing yellow bear Brakes-and-Alignment sign. Out of the truck, Bo turned to thank the driver, but "Ain't none of *yours*, neither" was fired back at him. The truck jumped forward, and Bo let the lurch shut the door. He walked to the garage-door window and peeked in: the yellow night-light was still burning, the workshop bench still scattered with tools and parts from the night before. The green Dodge was gone.

Musta done somethin' right, he thought, they drove her away.

Neither Enoch nor wrecker were in sight. The portent of Bill's attack hit home: Enoch was up to tricks again, but only the men were supposed to know. "Not even the angels in heaven shall know the hour of his coming." Bo laughed as he entered the oppressive smell of red clay, grease, and gasoline. He straightened the tool bench, washed, locked up, and headed for Lucy's.

The boardinghouse was ugly. It loomed three stories straight up from the flat hollow-basin, as plain and ponderous as the great boulders Bo had seen on TV westerns. Noise echoed through its walls; sounds of plumbing malfunctions and boarder disagreements. On the back, a lean-to had been converted into a dinette.

Inside, Bo rediscovered the aromas of breakfast. Ten miners were eating; Lucy was packing their lunches in arch-topped tin boxes. Bo swaggered to the jukebox, punched F-6 in defiant remembrance of Bill, and sauntered to the counter. But nobody had watched as he thought they would have. Ike Turner's bass voice chanted the rhythm; Tina whispered in.

Lucy coldly asked if he wanted coffee. He did not answer, but got his coffee anyway. The miners left and the straw bosses came down. Unlike their men, who whispered labor and safety secrets, the straw bosses ate alone and silently.

Bo, withdrawn, watched them. He wondered why he could not claim kin to men by tolerating their music, their cards, their fox hunting, but he knew a scab of indifference to keep away sociability.

When the foremen left, Lucy refilled Bo's cup. Too many color treatments had left her hair the same red as a rusty Brillo pad. She wore only a hint of green eye-makeup, and her skin was the texture and color of toadstools. On each hand she wore a diamond engagement ring. Bet ya can still throw 'em, Bo thought.

"How's goin', Bo?" She meant it, and that was appealing.

"Ain't too clear on it, Lucy. Bored, I guess."

"Try a different song tomorrow."

"Tomorrow's Sunday. 'Sides, I ain't bored with my song."

"How old are you again?"

"Sixteen, last count."

"Took sixteen years to bore ya?"

"Took that long to take effect."

Lucy laughed. Bo watched her face contort, wondered if she was laughing with him or at him, decided that was why the other men called her a whore, and smiled.

"You look hell-bottom low. Somethin' eatin' at ya? Yer momma sick er somethin'?"

"Nobody wants to talk to me, Lucy."

"Quit cryin' in yer coffee. You ain't old enough to be a blubberin' drunk."

"Well, it's the truth."

"Got a girl?"

"Had one this summer. Her daddy moved off to Logan. We wrote, only I don't hear much since school started up again."

Lucy remembered growing up. "Yer okay. Just growin' pains."

"I guess it's just I don't say nothin' worth listenin' to."

"Bo, listenin's worth more to the listener."

He would remember to look for meaning later; he sought another avenue of talk, but Lucy was too quick.

"Case of the lonesomes, huh?"

"Yeah."

"Must be pretty bad if your best talker's a whore."

Bo hung his head and waited for the roof to fall. When it didn't, he slowly added support.

"You ain't that," he said, looking as serious as he could without looking stupid.

Lucy searched for hand business, and found ten seconds in

turning off the grill and wiping up a drop of coffee. "I like it . . . you sayin' that. Yer the only one to believe it. Could be right good for ya. Could be dangerous. Don't go talkin' it around, hear?"

Bo shrugged. "Sure, Lucy," he said, withdrawing to his scab and his coffee. He watched her clear the straw-bosses' tables, showing bits of garter each time she bent. He rubbed his finger around the rim of the empty cup.

"How about another, Lucy?" he asked, as she bent long over a table to get at the corner. She smiled in a vague, sleepy way as she tugged her skirt down from her hips.

"Sure, Bo," she said, moving behind the counter for the pot, and added, "Past time for work," as she poured. "When the cat's away . . ."

"Cat's been doin' some playin' on his own."

"Huh?"

Bo gave Lucy the dime, then placed a quarter under the saucer. Nobody tipped Lucy, which compelled Bo to do it. The tip was a game between them, a secret. All the coffee Bo could drink for thirty-five cents.

As he slid from the stool, Lucy asked, "What's the rush? Tired of talkin'?"

"Need to look through the junk pile. Parts for my car. Gonna break out like gangbusters."

"Take me with ya."

"Sure," he said for the sake of play, and stepped out into the creeping shade of morning. Somehow he thought of how fine he felt in a new way, a knowing way.

It was nearly nine when Enoch came in. Bo lay on a crawler under Beck Fuller's Pontiac, draining excretions from the crankcase and twisting a filthy rag around the grease tits to remove warts of clay.

"Be a damn sight easier on the lift," Enoch grumbled. Bo avoided the hole. He was forbidden to use the lift.

He scooted the crawler into the light, shoved his welder's beanie back, and studied Enoch. Everything in the man's posture had slipped to the lowest support. His jaws drooped, dragging the scalp tight on his close-cropped head. His belly pulled the same way against whatever power was left in his shoulders. All of this converged on his khaki pants, making the cuffs gather in little bundles at his feet.

"Don't mind the work. Only thing doin' all mornin'. Where ya been at?"

Enoch lit a cigarette. "Checkin' out a wreck. Dawn Reed and Anne Davis went off the road up by French Creek Church. Car rolled int' the creek. Found 'em dead 'smornin'." He smiled at Bo, but Bo did not smile back. "Wasn't they 'bout your age?" he sputtered.

Bo stood up and brushed his jeans. "Jesus, yes. I go to school with 'em. Drunk?"

"Don't know yet. They was full of water. All scrunged up like raisins.

"Hey, her car was an Impala. I dropped it up to my house till the state cops are done with it. I'll sell ya parts real cheap. It ain't the same year as yours, but you could —"

"No thanks." Bo's stomach contracted, his nose, ears, and hands felt cold. Enoch cocked his head in wonder, took another draw from his cigarette, and turned away.

"Yer crazy," he said, turning back. "Just nuts. *They — are — dead.* Got that? Don't need no car no more." He turned again to ward off fury. Bo traced a stick figure in the Pontiac's dust with his finger, then wiped it out again. Another preachin', he thought.

"I come in here 'smornin' to get that miner's Dodge out," Enoch said. "Them tools was ever'where. You wasn't nowhere. Sleepin'? Sleep more'n ya work. Snuck in t' put 'em away while I's down to the station. Figger Bill wouldn't tell me you's at that whore's house?"

"She ain't that," Bo whispered, looking for something to throw at Enoch.

"She ain't, huh? Well, how do you think she got that board-in'house? Bartram didn't give it to her — she blackmailed 'im for it the way she done them other guys in Charleston. You stay clear of her, Bo, she'll ruin ya."

"Don't tell me what to do," Bo shouted.

"I gotta watch out for my interests. You work for me, you stay outa that house."

"I quit!" he shouted so loudly his throat hurt. He threw his rag in the barrel for effect, adding, "I got enough on you to earn my keep without workin'." Half out the door the lie frightened him; he wanted to turn back, blame Lucy, and keep his chance to leave forever. You blew it, something whispered, but pride pointed his way outside.

Inside, Enoch worried. Bo was probably lying. But what if he knew about him and the boys and Dawn? He looked up the road, but Bo was walking too fast to catch on foot. Enoch ground the wrecker to a start and whirled off up the road.

As the wrecker pulled up beside him, Bo set his jaw in silence. He looked at Enoch, and the flabby jaws said, "Git in, Bo, we gotta talk." Once he had Bo inside, Enoch let the subject of blackmail sleep, and went on with his sermon:

"I know'd your daddy. That's why I give ya this job. You're a good mechanic, but you proved you ain't no man by walkin' out on me.

"I tried to be good to ya. Let you use my tools on yer car, even teached you how to be a mechanic . . . but I can't teach ya how to be a man."

"Try treatin' me like one," Bo hissed.

"All right. You want to work? Your daddy wouldn't want me

to let ya after the way you acted. I'm sorry to his memory, but I'll let you come back."

Bo looked out on the broom-sedge slopes. He could swear his daddy's ghost answered, "Yech."

"All right," said Enoch. "Tonight we're goin' fox huntin'. I figger yer daddy woulda took ya by now."

Bo hated fox hunting, but nodded and smiled. He wanted his job; he'd need a stake.

When he had finished servicing Beck's car, Bo washed his hands, lit a cigarette, and waited to become hungry. Enoch had said he would be back, but Bo was glad to be alone.

Dawn and Anne were dead. He boiled memories of them in his mind. Dawn was chesty and popular. She was dumb, but smart enough to act smart. Bo respected and spoke to her. Anne was built so slightly she always wore white blouses so onlookers could tell she had a bra, and therefore something to hold up. Her only friend was Dawn, her only beauty was in her eyes. She'd never stare down a husband, Bo thought, so maybe it's best. Dawn brushed against him a lot, not always so he would notice, but enough to make him wonder what she had meant.

Bo leaned his head against the red battery-charger and closed his eyes on Dawn's memory, while a vision of Lucy rocked smiling in his brain.

He saw a clapboard house, worn silver by weather, now glistening in the sun. He felt the intruder-sun on his head and the power he loved coax him toward the cool shade of the house. He saw movement up the moss-green sandstone steps, across the grooved porch-floor, and through the screen door. In the cool dampness of the linoleum living room, his cousin Sally stood; her hair pressed in ragged bangs on her forehead, the rest pinned loosely behind. Little chains of grime made sweaty chokers around her throat, but she looked cool and remote as she moved toward him and took his hand. "I don't love you," he said, viciously. Images soon ran together in flesh tones, and he awakened.

The dream had excited him as the cold August rain blowing through a porch might break the monotony of heat and pleasure-chill his blood. He searched for a reason for the dream. Maybe, he thought, I made it up. Maybe it happened.

Hunger drove him beyond Enoch's Law, and he ran quickly to the dinette. The door was locked, so he dragged himself to Brownie's, where he bought cheese, crackers, pork-rind snacks, and two Big Orange drinks.

"Dolla-fourtee." Bo handed the old man the money, tore into the cheese and Big Orange. "Don't eat it here," Brownie added, bagging the lunch.

Bo sat outside the garage in the cold sun and ate. He watched the Duncan sisters as they sat by their window and watched him with peeping sparrow-eyes. When he had drained the last Big Orange, he felt a wickedness rise in him as he chucked the empty bottle at the Duncan house, and he smiled to see them retreat behind their curtains.

Enoch returned at two-twenty, found Bo asleep against the battery charger. Cuffy had suggested cutting Bo's throat, and now was the time, but Cuffy was not around, and Enoch was not a cutter of throats.

"Wake up, Bo, goddammit, wake yourself up."

"Wha?"

"Look, I'm goin' to get the dogs. You lock up at three, an' be on the road afront of your house by six. I'll get ya there."

"Who alls comin'?" Bo yawned.

"Cuffy an' Bill an' Virg Cooper."

"Cuffy an' Bill don't like me," he warned.

"Don't be a smart-ass an' they will. Dress warm, hear?"

Bo nodded, thinking, son of a bitch.

He waited until Enoch's wrecker silhouetted the grade and passed over, then he locked up and headed for Lucy's. She sat alone reading a magazine and looking day-worn. Maybe she caught a man, Bo thought, but he threw her back. Over coffee he poured out his roil of sickness, hate, and confusion. Soon they were wrestling with the go or don't-go of the hunt.

"Bo, ya drive people off an' dump 'em. Go ahuntin' — they're just tryin' to be good to ya."

He looked up sternly. "You don't kick a dog in the ass then give 'im a bone."

Then with a sudden fervor: "Maybe I could take Daddy's forty-five automatic."

"Can't shoot foxie, Bo," she warned. "Be nothin' left to chase."

"I know," he said, as if a veteran of hunts. "I just want to show 'em I can shoot. You know, plug some cans."

"Make damn sure them cans ain't got legs," she grinned.

He gulped his coffee and left so quickly he forgot to leave his tip.

The clay trail from the secondary to Bo's hillside house was worn a smooth red in the center, bordered with a yellow crust. He followed the path into the perpetual dusk and sweet-chill of a pine grove. There the path forked, one toward the garbage pile, the other into a clearing where the house stood, rudely shingled in imitation-brick tar paper.

The clearing was scattered with pin-oak and sugar-maple leaves lodged in fallow weeds. The sugar maples blended their colors to camouflage the undying plastic daffodils his mother had planted around the porch.

Bo panicked when he saw the shedded skin of a copperhead on the porch steps, then laughed at the dusty suggestion, bounced on it daringly, and up to the porch. He opened the whining screen door, burst the jammed wooden door open, and heard his mother: " 'Sat you, Bo?" He remembered how she used to call him her "only Bo." As a boy he had liked it; now it made him shudder. But it didn't matter; she no longer called him in that fashion.

"Yeah, Momma."

As he washed his hands at the sink, he looked out the kitchen window at the heap in the backyard. It was slowly becoming a '66 Impala again. "Like gangbusters," he had said to Lucy, then asked himself, "When?" Turning his attention to his soap-lathered hands dissolved the question, but another sprang in its place: Why not use Dawn's car as a parts department?

He tried to find peace in cooking, but while he chopped potatoes and onions into the skillet, he heard his mother stirring in the bedroom. The aroma of pork grease had reached her, and she shouted, "Smells good." Instead of answering, Bo turned to sawing chops from a whole loin. These he fried also, not turning them until the blood oozed out and turned gray in the skillet.

His mother slipped into the kitchen with short, uneasy steps and dropped into the cushioned chair by the table. She had been resting. The doctor told her to rest eight years ago, when her husband died. Miner's insurance paid her to rest until the rest sapped her strength.

She leaned a tired, graying, but still-brown head of hair against the wall, and let her eyelids sag complacently. She wore two print cotton dresses — one over the other. Two-dress fall, Bo thought, means a three-dress-and-coat winter.

Bo put the food on the table and was about to shovel pork into his mouth when his mother asked for her medicine. "It's in the winder above the sink."

"Has been for eight years," said Bo, scooting his chair out. As he gathered the bottles of colored pills, his glance went once again to the car. The tires were flat.

"I need my medicine," said his mother, while mashing her food into a mush between the fork prongs. She spoke over a mouthful: "When you gonna junk that thing like your Momma ast?"

"Never," he said, setting the bottles and himself at the table. "Probably die workin' on it. Enoch's got . . ." He did not want to mention the wreck at supper.

"Enoch's got what?"

"Got some parts, but I need more."

"It'll get snakes next spring."

"It al's gets snakes, and I al's run 'em off. Now will you leave my car be?"

"TV movie looks like a good 'un tonight," she said in penance.

"Gotta date at the dance in Helvetia."

When the supper dishes were finished, Bo dressed quickly while his mother rested from the walk back to the bedroom. Once wrapped, he slipped to the hall closet and took the .45 from its hatbox. He checked the clip: it was loaded with brightly oiled brass shells. The gun even smelled good. Shoving the weapon into his pocket, he shouted, "Night, Momma," and heard her whimper instructions as he closed and locked the door.

The sun was not setting, nor was it seen. It hid behind the western slopes so only a hint of sun rose upward, firing the ridges with a green fire, and leaving everything in the hollow a clean, cold shadow. Bo knew a freeze was coming. It was too cold to snow. He would have to go now.

Bo watched the trees and houses go by as he only half-listened to Enoch's chatter about his two blueticks, Mattingly and Moore.

"Now Matt, he knows how to run, but Moore can figger if a fox is throwed the pack and he knows just where to look for him."

Bo thought: "I shoulda stayed and watched that movie. Wish Spanker hadn'ta run off. Couldn't stand to be tied up, though."

Houses and tales drifted by. Bo looked back at Matt and Moore, wobbly legged and motion sick.

"I was younger'n you the first time my daddy taked me ahuntin'." Enoch shifted down, and the transmission rattled like a bucket of chains. "Got drunk on two spoons of shine an' half a chew. Man. That was a time. Sittin' back . . . listen to them ol' honkers, and sittin' back. I growed up quick. Had to to stay alive. You ever know my daddy?"

"Nope," said Bo, thinking, wonder what that movie was.

"Your daddy knowed 'im. Meaner'n a teased snake. Got me laid when I's eight. Took me t' a house in Clarksburg — ol' gal said I couldn't come in — so he left me in the car an' went back with a tire tool — then he come an' got me an' showed me that ol' gal an' her man conked out on the floor."

"Musta been some excitement," Bo said, looking at the patterns trees threw against the sky as the truck passed.

"Yeah, an' that ain't all. He taked me t' this room an' busted in on this gal an' made her lay real still till I's finished. Then she called Daddy a SOB cause all he give her was fifty cents, an' he knocked her teeth out."

Enoch laughed wildly, but Bo only smiled. Old Man Enoch was dead, but the rumors of strangers' graves found in pigpens still grew.

"When'd ya git yer first?"

Bo told the afternoon dream as a fact, adding color and characters as he went until he was only inches out of shotgun range when "the sweet thing's old man cut down on me with his sixteen-gauge."

"Damn, who was she?"

"Think I'd tell you so's you could go an' tell on me an' get me killed?"

"Just never figgered you for the type. Guess I been takin' you all wrong." Enoch added in consideration: "Yer pretty slick."

Once they topped the hill, small slashes of light broke through the trees; enough to see rabbits and the road without headlights. Bo was about to mention his gun, but they pulled so quickly off the timber trail, he forgot it. The truck rumbled into a small room in the forest: it was walled with trees, hearthed by a pit of cold ashes, and furnished with broken car-seats. Now, Bo thought, climbing from the truck. Now loose. Alone. Smell power in the air — smells like good metal in temper. Dawn never brush against me again. Alone.

"Git some firewood," Enoch ordered.

Bo swung around. "Look, I work for you from the time I git there till when I leave. You want somethin' t'night, better ask like a friend."

"Cocky, ain't ya?"

"I gotta right."

"You ain't actin' like a man."

"You ain't treatin' me like one."

Bo and Enoch combed the littered hill for shed-wood and abandoned timber.

Two miles beyond, an owl watched a meadow from the branches of a dead hickory tree. Hidden in the underbrush, the fox watched the owl and the meadow. Both saw the rabbit meandering through the dying ironweed and goldenrod, and both waited for the best condition of attack. When the moment came, the owl was on wing before the fox had lifted a pad.

The wind changed, and the fox changed cover while keeping close watch on the feasting owl. The fox crept carefully, judged the distance to the nearest cover, then rushed the owl with a bark. The bird flew straight up in alarm, aimed at the thief, and dropped, only to bury its talons in ironweed and earth. Fox and prey were under cover, leaving the bird robbed and hungry in the silver dusk.

Bo built a fire while Enoch tended the dogs. Mattingly and Moore sniffed the air as they overcame their sickness. They pranced and bit the chains as Enoch checked their feet for stones or cuts. As the fire came to life, Bo felt a baseness growing within himself, felt he knew the forest better than the man with the dogs, and, for a moment, wanted to run into the darkness.

Bill began to honk his horn at the foot of the hill and continued to honk his way up the hill trail. The dogs barked from the pain in their ears. "Drunk already," Enoch shouted, laughing. Under a persimmon bush, the fox gnawed rabbit bones and rested, pausing between chews to listen.

The truck lunged into camp; Cuffy fell out, the other men stumbling behind, leaving the frothing dogs tied to the bed of the truck.

"What the hell's he doin' here?" said Cuffy, pointing at Bo.

"I invited him," Enoch said.

"Hey, Enoch," shouted Virg, looking from man to dog and back again. "You an' Matt are beginnin' to look alike."

Cuffy sauntered to the fire, took the seat opposite Bo, and they eyed each other with disgust.

"Wha's Nutsy doin' here?" he taunted.

"I like it here," Bo fired back.

"Don't git too used to it."

Bo left Cuffy to join the group.

"B'god, don' tell me that dog can run," Enoch yelled at Bill.

"Bender's the best runner. Bet he sings first *and* leads 'em," Bill answered.

"I'll bet on Moore to sing out first," said Bo. "And Bender to lead."

"Least you got *half* a brain," said Bill.

"How much?" asked Bo.

"Dollar."

"Done," said Bo. Enoch bet Bill on his own, and they shook hands all around before releasing the dogs.

The men brought out their bourbon, and Enoch gave Bo a

special present — moonshine in a mason jar. Then they retired to the fire to swap tales until trail broke.

From his post in the brush the fox could hear sniffing searches being carried out. Dabbing his paws in rabbit gore for a head start, he darted over the bank toward the hollow. Queen, Bill's roan hound, was first to find the trail. Instead of calling, she cut back across the ridge to where cold trail told her he was prone to cross. Moore sang out lowly as he sniffed to distinguish fox from rabbit.

"Moore," Enoch shouted, "I'd know 'im anyplace."

"Dog's keen-mouthed all right," said Virg.

Bill paid each man the dollar he owed.

"Made a mistake about that boy," Enoch bragged, embarrassing Bo. "Tell 'em 'bout yer first woman, Bo." The men leaned forward, looking at Bo.

"You tell 'em, Enoch, I ain't drunk enough."

Bo corrected Enoch's rehash from time to time as the listeners hooted their approving laughter.

"Fred said he couldn't go ahuntin'," said Cuffy, watching Bo for some reaction. "Seems somebody's been messin' whit his wife whilst he's gone." Bo stared Cuffy down, then took a full drink from his jar.

"Maybe 'twas that hippie back of Fred," Virg offered.

"Hippie just screws animals," said Cuffy.

"Or other hippies," Enoch added.

"That's what he means," Bo explained, and they all broke into a wild wind of laughter.

The last of the firewood was burning when Bill was finishing his tale. The dogs had been forgotten.

"Like I said, we's all drunk an' Cuffy an' Tom got to argyin' 'bout the weight of them two hogs . . . had 'em all clean and butchered an' packed. Them two bastards loaded 'em on the truck —

guts an' all — an' took 'em to Sutton to weigh 'em. Got the guts all mixed up, an' fit ober what head went to what hog."

"Weren't much kick to that hog when I gutted 'im," Cuffy reminisced.

" 'Bout like you kicked when they brained you," Virg spouted. And the men belched laughter again.

The fox was climbing the trail to camp, the pack trailing behind. Queen waited in the brush near the men, cold-trail sure the fox would cross here. The fox circled trees, his last trick to lose the pack.

Bo was woven into the gauze-light, torn between passing out and taking another drink. He caught bits of conversation, then his mind drifted into hollow sleep, and the voices jerked him awake again.

"He's sittin' in the Holy Seat," said Bill's voice in Bo's darkness. Bo kept his eyes closed.

"That was one helluva wreck," said Enoch. "Way I figger it, she drowned."

"Whycome?" asked Virg.

"She was all wrinkly — sorta scrunged up."

"The Holy Pole is in your hold, so work yer ass to save your soul," Cuffy proclaimed.

"She was damn good, all right." Enoch's voice drifted away.

"Hell," said Virg, "I al's went last."

"First come, first served," said Bill.

"Shut up," said Cuffy. "I'm horny again."

"Hell, we all are," said Virg. "Let's dig her up."

"Maybe she's still warm," added Cuffy. The men giggled until they were coughing.

"Told her old man she had a job," Enoch laughed.

"I miss her," sighed Virg.

"I don't," shouted Cuffy. "She coulda hung us all if'n somebody didn' marry her. Nosir, I'm glad she's dead."

Bo fingered the .45 in his pocket.

But the men had whittled the time away telling lies mingled with truth until Bo could no longer distinguish between the two. He had told things, too; no truth or lie could go untold. It was fixed now; the truth and lies were all told.

The fox broke through the clearing, pausing at the sight of fire and man. Queen burst to attack just as the confused fox retreated toward her. There was a yelp, and the fox dashed for the hollow with Queen running a sight chase.

"That damn cutter," Bill shouted. Bo drunkenly swung the .45 from his coat pocket, shot at Queen, and missed. Cuffy screamed as the shot echoed from the dark western ridges. Queen paused to look at Bo, then went back to trail. Virg jumped up and kicked the gun from Bo's hand.

"Try'n save foxie," Bo slurred.

"You stupid son of a bitch," said Cuffy, and Bo looked for the pistol to kill him, but it was lost in the leaves and darkness. His head throbbed, and he looked stupidly at the men.

"Leave 'im alone," said Enoch. "Nobody never teached 'im no better."

Bo stood wavering, and said to Virg, "I's sorry, but I's tryin' to save foxie."

Cuffy spat on Bo's shoe, but he ignored it, walked to the bushes, and threw up.

"You guys piss on the fire," said Enoch. "I'll call the dogs."

Bo nearly missed the clearing in the strange, misty-gray light of Sunday afternoon. Dried oak leaves whispered in the sapless branches above him, and an autumn-blooming flower hung limply on its stem, frostbitten for its rebellion.

The remnants of the night lay strewn about the leaf-floor like a torpid ghost. The mason jar was empty, but his head felt fine — only an ache of change, like a cold coming on. He could smell cold ashes and vomit in the air, but the molten smell was gone from the wind, or perhaps the wind had carried it on.

He found his father's pistol, laced with rusty lines from the wet leaves, and shoved it into his coat pocket. As he lurched down the clay timber-trail toward the secondary, he wondered if the Impala would be ready to roll by spring.

✹

TIME AND AGAIN

M R. Weeks called me out again tonight, and I look back
down the hall of my house. I left the kitchen light burning. This is an empty old house since the old lady died. When Mr.
Weeks doesn't call, I write everybody I know about my boy.
Some of my letters always come back, and the folks who write back
say nobody knows where he got off to. I can't help but think he
might come home at night when I am gone, so I let the kitchen
light burn and go on out the door.

The cold air is the same, and the snow pellets my cap, sifts under
my collar. I hear my hogs come grunting from their shed, thinking I have come to feed them. I ought to feed them better than
that awful slop, but I can't until I know my boy is safe. I told
him not to go and look, that the hogs just squeal because I never
kill them. They always squeal when they are happy, but he went
and looked. Then he ran off someplace.

I brush the snow from my road plow's windshield and climb
in. The vinyl seats are cold, but I like them. They are smooth
and easy cleaned. The lug wrench is where it has always been
beside my seat. I heft it, put it back. I start the salt spreader,
lower my shear, and head out to clean the mountain road.

The snow piles in a wall against the berm. No cars move. They
are stranded at the side, and as I plow past them, a line falls in
behind me, but they always drop back. They don't know how long

83

it takes the salt to work. They are common fools. They rush around in such weather and end up dead. They never sit still and wait for the salt to work.

I think I am getting too old to do this anymore. I wish I could rest and watch my hogs get old and die. When the last one is close to dying, I will feed him his best meal and leave the gate open. But that will most likely not happen, because I know this stretch of Route 60 from Ansted to Gauley, and I do a good job. Mr. Weeks always brags on what a good job I do, and when I meet the other truck plowing the uphill side of this road, I will honk. That will be Mr. Weeks coming up from Gauley. I think how I never met Mr. Weeks in my life but in a snowplow. Sometimes I look out to Sewel Mountain and see snow coming, then I call Mr. Weeks. But we are not friends. We don't come around each other at all. I don't even know if he's got family.

I pass the rest stop at Hawks Nest, and a new batch of fools line up behind me, but pretty soon I am alone again. As I plow down the grade toward Chimney Corners, my lights are the only ones on the road, and the snow takes up the yellow spinning of my dome light and the white curves of my headlights. I smile at the pretties they make, but I am tired and wish I was home. I worry about the hogs. I should have given them more slop, but when the first one dies, the others will eat him quick enough.

I make the big turn at Chimney Corners and see a hitchhiker standing there. His front is clean, and he looks half frozen, so I stop to let him in.

He says, "Hey, thank you, Mister."

"How far you going?"

"Charleston."

"You got family there?" I say.

"Yessir."

"I only go to Gauley Bridge, then I turn around."

"That's fine," he says. He is a polite boy.

The fools pack up behind me, and my low gears whine away from them. Let them fall off the mountain for all I care.

"This is not good weather to be on the road," I say.

"Sure ain't, but a fellow's got to get home."

"Why didn't you take a bus?"

"Aw, buses stink," he says. My boy always talked like that.

"Where you been?"

"Roanoke. Worked all year for a man. He give me Christmastime and a piece of change."

"He sounds like a good man."

"You bet. He's got this farm outside of town — horses — you ain't seen such horses. He's gonna let me work the horses next year."

"I have a farm, but I only have some hogs left."

"Hogs is good business," he says.

I look at him. "You ever see a hog die?" I look back at the road snow.

"Sure."

"Hogs die hard. I seen people die in the war easier than a hog at a butchering."

"Never noticed. We shot and stuck them pretty quick. They do right smart jerking around, but they're dead by then."

"Maybe."

"What can you do with a hog if you don't butcher him? Sell him?"

"My hogs are old hogs. Not good for anything. I just been letting them die. I make my money on this piece of road every winter. Don't need much."

He says, "Ain't got any kids?"

"My boy run off when my wife died. But that was considerable time ago."

He is quiet a long time. Where the road is patched, I work my shear up, and go slower to let more salt hit behind. In my mirror, I see the lights of cars sneaking up behind me.

Then of a sudden the hitchhiker says, "What's your boy do now?"

"He was learning a mason's trade when he run off."

"Makes good money."

"I don't know. He was only a hod carrier then."

He whistles. "I done that two weeks this summer. I never been so sore."

"It's hard work," I say. I think, this boy has good muscles if he can carry hod.

I see the lights of Mr. Weeks's snowplow coming toward us. I gear into first. I am not in a hurry. "Scrunch down," I say. "I'd get in trouble for picking you up."

The boy hunkers in the seat, and the lights from Mr. Weeks's snowplow shine into my cab. I wave into the lights, not seeing Mr. Weeks, and we honk when we pass. Now I move closer to center. I want to do a good job and get all the snow, but when the line of cars behind Mr. Weeks comes toward me, I get fidgety. I don't want to cause any accidents. The boy sits up and starts talking again, and it makes me jittery.

"I was kinda scared about coming through Fayette County," he says.

"Uh-huh," I say. I try not to brush any cars.

"Damn, but a lot of hitchhikers gets killed up here."

A man lays on his horn as he goes past, but I have to get what Mr. Weeks left, and I am always too close to center.

The boy says, "That soldier's bones — Jesus, but that was creepy."

The last car edges by, but my back and shoulders are shaking and I sweat.

"That soldier," he says. "You know about that?"

"I don't know."

"They found his duffel bag at the bottom of Lovers' Leap. All his grip was in there, and his bones, too."

"I remember. That was too bad." The snow makes such nice pictures in my headlights, and it rests me to watch them.

"There was a big retard got killed up here, too. He was the only one they ever found with all his meat on. Rest of them, they just find their bones."

"They haven't found any in years," I say. This snow makes me think of France. It was snowing like this when they dropped us over France. I yawn.

"I don't know," he says. "Maybe the guy who done them all in is dead."

"I figure so," I say.

The hill bottoms out slowly, and we drive on to Gauley, clearing the stretch beside New River. The boy is smoking and taking in the snow.

"It snowed like this in France the winter of 'forty-four," I say. "I was in the paratroops, and they dropped us where the Germans were thick. My platoon took a farmhouse without a shot."

"Damn," he says. "Did you knife them?"

"Snapped their necks," I say, and I see my man tumble into the sty. People die so easy.

We come to Gauley, where the road has already been cleared by the other trucks. I pull off, and the line of cars catches up, sloshing by. I grip the wrench.

"Look under the seat for my flashlight, boy."

He bends forward, grabbing under the seat, and his head is turned from me. But I am way too tired now, and I don't want to clean the seat.

"She ain't there, Mister."

"Well," I say. I look at the lights of the cars. They are fools.

"Thanks again," he says. He hops to the ground, and I watch

him walking backward, thumbing. I am almost too tired to drive home. I sit and watch this boy walking backward until a car stops for him. I think, he is a polite boy, and lucky to get rides at night.

All the way up the mountain, I count the men in France, and I have to stop and count again. I never get any farther than that night it snowed. Mr. Weeks passes me and honks, but I don't honk. Time and again, I try to count and can't.

I pull up beside my house. My hogs run from their shelter in the backyard and grunt at me. I stand by my plow and look at the first rims of light around Sewel Mountain through the snowy limbs of the trees. Cars hiss by on the clean road. The kitchen light still burns, and I know the house is empty. My hogs stare at me, snort beside their trough. They are waiting for me to feed them, and I walk to their pen.

✹

THE MARK

ON the morning of the fair the smell came to Reva in the kitchen, slicing through the thick odors of coffee and fish roe. She left the dishes and carried her coffee through the tunneling light of the hallway, past her brother's neatly framed arrowheads, past the charcoal portrait of her grandfather, beyond the cool darkness, onto the porch. The land and river were hidden under a thick brown fog that the sun was peeling away. The fog smelled of ore and earth, and Reva sat to breathe it in, rubbing weariness from the bones in her hands. She felt thick with worry for her brother; working the same river that had killed their parents only eight years ago. The worry was making one of her spells come, and she promised herself to forget.

In the yard, chuckleheaded Jackie, the tenant, curried Tyler's prize bull, singing some idiot's tune quietly. The bull shifted his huge weight from side to side, shuddering against the unnatural ripples Jackie's brush had put into his black fur. As "the Pride and Promise of Cutter's Landing" whipped his ropish tail against early flies, Reva mocked, "Peeepeee," before sipping her coffee. The bull shifted again.

"Holt still, damn ya," Jackie grunted, losing his song.

Peepee, Reva grinned to herself. Pea-brained Peepee pees on his heifers. Peeepeee.

Tyler, her husband, came to the porch wearing his green plaid shirt and blue trousers.

"This okay?" he asked, modeling in a pivot.

"For a sideshow, yeah," she laughed.

"I can't help it," he said, embarrassed for his color blindness.

"Find the light-colored slacks, Big T.," she said, knowing they were tan, and watched him shuffle down the hall like a little boy, and not her husband of two winters.

She felt the spot where the baby should be, closed her eyes, and tried to imagine her blood in the rabbit's veins. It would pump into the ovaries, making them swell, the doctor had said, if she was pregnant. They were going to kill the rabbit and look for her secret in its organs, but the sinkings in her belly came on too hard and frightening, too much like her worst month. She told herself they would find no confessions in the rabbit ovaries.

She remembered her brother Clinton holding a litter of baby rabbits close to his naked chest while the mowing machine droned behind him in a dead hum. Was that the summer she began to want him?

She looked to where the fog had lifted away from the road and was crossing the acres of tobacco in the river bottom, leaving a glistening coat of dew. Clinton had helped them top and worm the crop before shipping out, and she squinted to think of a whore holding her brother's strong body, smelling the smoky scent of their grandfather. By next week there would be only dry stubble for snakes to shed in, and a dusty smell from the crackling curing-barn.

Tyler came back in light-blue jeans, a pair Reva had forgotten. She took a deep breath of the August heat.

"What the hell's Jackie up to?" he asked, watching the tenant.

Reva did not answer. A grasshopper landed on the banister, and Reva watched its armored jaws bubble juice. On the same spot, once, her grandfather had told his boatman's tales and sung the chanteys, and she had traded dark secrets with her brother.

"Go on an' put him in the truck, Jackie," Tyler shouted, then murmured, "Goddamn ignoramus'll just have to do it all over at the fair. But he does look down right champeen, don't he? Even had Jackie polish his ring."

"Don't that beat all," she said, going to fetch the pants herself.

"Yessir," Tyler said to the bull, "you look downright elegant."

Coming back through the hallway, Reva locked eyes with the stare of her grandfather but, not knowing his young face, kept her pace to the porch.

"Go put these on 'fore Bill an' Carlene gets here," she said, handing Tyler the trousers.

"Don't ya wanta help?" he said, hooking his arm around her waist and grinning as he kissed her neck. He smelled of Aqua Velva, but his chin was rough.

"You missed a spot," she said, brushing her hand across his face and pushing away. He went into the house.

Jackie goaded "Pride and Promise" into the straight-bed truck, tied him, and latched the gate. Reva watched him hang his chuckled head as he jogged to the barn, knock-kneed. She wondered if he had a bottle hidden there.

The fog was gone, and she could see the hills beyond the river — hills that soon gave way to the plains of Ohio. On the eastern shore, nearly hidden in the vines and weeds, stood the ship-lapped wooden lockhouse where her grandfather once worked. Even as it stood empty in their youth, it had been her playhouse or Clinton's fort. By its concrete foundation, they dug for the bones of a body their grandfather said he had fished from the river as a boy, but never found them. Up and down the shore, paths were worn slick in the black river-clay. On the smooth gray bark of a water maple, its roots breaking the abutment of a lock gate, Clinton had carved their parents' initials on the cold December Friday the bridge collapsed.

A small dusty breeze moved across the porch, and Reva shivered in its heat, closing her eyes to tears from staring too long. A tiny pain screwed into her back, and she tried to hate against being left here, alone. She tried to blame Clinton, her parents, even the river, but opened her eyes to the white knuckles of her tiny fist.

The bull stomped indifferently in the truck bed, and the early sun warmed the locust into buzzing, but the good air had gone with the fog. When she saw Bill's new Buick turn off the highway, she got up heavily and went inside.

☘

"She stares 'bout all the time," Tyler said, watching the bull, waiting for his brother's answer.

The brother sat slightly higher on the banister, smoking. The locust buzz only thickened the air, and the dusty leaves of the water-maple hills hung limp green, showing no flags of wind. Bill yawned.

Tyler looked up at his brother. "I figgered I'd give her a baby to keep her mind offa Clint. Boy, she was ripe the day he left. Now she just misses that sassy talk of his."

Bill still said nothing, and Tyler got up to stand beside his brother. Bill scratched at Tyler's worry.

"Aw shit, T., quit worryin' like some ol' woman. You got a farm to work. Worry 'bout that."

"Sure 'nough there. Weren't for that tobacca yonder, I'd be up shit creek."

Reva stood in the hallway, her index finger tracing the serrated edge of a rose-colored arrowhead. Clinton had called it a Shawnee war-point, and gave it center honor because it was her favorite. Upstairs the toilet flushed, and she heard her sister-in-law humming as she primped. She went out.

92

"Ready?" Tyler said, springing off the steps.

"Where's Carlene?" Bill asked.

"In the john, I have an idee," she said, snapping her purse closed.

"Wife's got a straight pipe," Bill said to his brother.

"Lookee there," Reva said, pointing to where a mole was tunneling in the yard. Tyler walked out and poised his heel over the moving earth.

"Tyler, that mole ain't botherin' us," she said, bored with her husband's grin.

"I know it," he said, dropping down at the head of the tunnel. "Dug his own grave."

"I heard tell ever'thin's poison on dog days," said Bill.

Reva shot him a cross look.

"What's poison?" said Carlene, coming to the porch.

"Nothin'." Reva brushed her hair back, then walked down the steps toward the Buick.

Jackie leaned against the truck, his big head lolling back on the sideboards. "Purty day," he said as Reva passed, and she nodded, smiling, knowing any sort of day was good for Jackie. Waiting in the car's building heat made the throb in her forehead bloom back between her ears. She stared at the sycamores and water maples along the riverbank. Secret totems hung there as gifts to the ghost-trees of her parents: a necklace from Reva, a charmed dog-bone from Clinton, bits of glass on fishing line to make the trees glitter in the winter sun. Her head cleared, and she heard the others coming to the car, whispering. Only Tyler's voice came up low from within him, ". . . but they been dead a long time."

In the silence of the car, Carlene felt bad about her sister-in-law's spells. She remembered Grandfather Cutter standing for weeks in the cold wind on the riverbank, watching the cars come up, water spewing from the lips of their torn metal. Only when rumor of a Ford truck met him would he move closer, watching. When his son's finally came up empty, he only walked to the truck where his grandchildren sat, staring at the masses of twisted steel.

The smooth blacktop was interrupted suddenly by a four-mile section of concrete slabs. The car jolted over each one as it passed, and Tyler slowed down, motioning Jackie to back off his tail.

"Damn idiot," he said, then, glancing into the mirror to where Bill sat behind him, "You seen Layman's bull, 'Rangoon'?"

"Sounds more like a disease," Bill chuckled.

"Probably got it in 'Nam."

"The name or the disease?" Reva grinned wickedly. No one laughed.

"I'll lay odds he made the papers on it," Tyler continued. "Good-looker without a line."

"Naw," Bill drawled, "Layman ain't that smart."

Carlene leaned forward to Reva. "I can't wait till ya hear from the doc. Scared?"

"Just mad," she said for Tyler's ears.

"Want a boy or a girl?" Carlene's blue eyes widened with her question.

"Don't matter. Just let it be till I know for sure."

Tyler took her hand, and she could feel the worry in his cold fingers. The ride was making her carsick, and she closed her eyes thinking Clinton might never come back after the baby was born.

"New Angus in the county," she heard Bill say, and felt Tyler's fingers flex.

"Whose?"

"Feller name of Jordan or Jergan — I forget, but the bull's called 'Imperial Sun' — S-u-n. All the way from Virginia."

"Good stock?"

"You couldn't afford the fee."

Carlene leaned up again. "What you gonna call the baby?"

"'Imperial Sun,'" Reva's voice was hollow.

"Ain't neither," Tyler tried to joke. "Gonna call him a'ter ol' Jeff D. Cutter. Ain't that so, Reva?"

"Sure, Big T."

"Who won last year?" Tyler looked at Bill's image, and waved Jackie back again.

"You know," Bill said, "I don't rightly recall."

❧

The FFA boy shifted his tobacco chew as he handed Reva her ham sandwich, smiling tightly against the juice in his mouth. With the afternoon sun in his eyes, his squint reminded her of her brother's, and she smiled back as she paid.

"I don't for the life of me know how ya eat that trash," Carlene sneered.

Remembering the boy's smile, Reva took a big bite and pulled a slice of meat from the sandwich. She wagged it at Carlene like a tongue, and her eyes brightened a little. "Good," Reva said, stuffing the meat into her mouth.

The sawdust midway was full of the scent of dirt and people and fun, not like the stock pens or stinking the same. As they strolled, they looked at blank faces gazing on their own. The children chased each other with shrieks and laughter. A redheaded boy was pulling mats of cotton candy from his hair while his sister slapped on more, laughing. On the bench, their mother stared into the forest of faces.

Reva remembered Clinton's teasings after her wedding. "Gonna get slapped down like a ol' catfish," he had said, laughing. Afterward, he had called her Catfish, and always warned her about beef bait and hooks before she went to Tyler's bed.

Again they passed the gut-jolting rides, and Carlene was edging toward the Dodg'em cars. "C'mon," she said.

"Naw, I been whipped up 'nough for today."

"Well, we done it all," Carlene said, disappointed.

"Ain't seen the sideshows nor the animals neither."

"Those?" Carlene snarled and squinted, but followed Reva down the midway to the shows.

Even with the barkers, the sideshow lane seemed quiet, and whispering adults made a drone below the barkers' calls. They passed the Monster of Calcutta and the Living Torch, listening as the whispers grew into voices when the shows cleared out. The stripper had no barker, needed none.

"Bill said she smokes a cigar with her you-know-what," Carlene whispered.

"Now that there's a trick," Reva answered. Her face lightened thinking about it. Her brother would come upriver, not in his boatman's clothes, but as a naked Indian hiding in the pawpaw tunnels. In the lockhouse she would show him that trick. Her mood shifted back when she thought some whore might already have shown him.

"Lookee, snakes," Reva shouted under her breath.

"Don't want to pay to see nothin' I got too much of."

"Aw c'mon, Carlene," Reva said, handing the barker her quarters. Carlene dragged behind, pushing through the crowd to where Reva had squeezed a place by the canvas-lined pit. In the pit among the harmless snakes sat a shoeless old man, his voice running on professionally, but laced with boredom.

"Now you can all see this is a living thing," he said, holding up a small snake. Then he dropped it down his throat. Carlene gagged, and the crowd whispered.

"You sir," he continued, pointing to a man in bib overalls, "do you see the snake hidden?" and he gaped his toothless jaws. The man in overalls did not look up, but shyly shook his head. The snake eater belched the snake into his hands and freed it to crawl with the others. Whispers rolled through the tent, but Reva followed Carlene outside. She felt sorry for Tyler and his mole-killing foot, but knew it would always be that way with him.

"I'm goin' back to the yards," Carlene said. "This here's makin' me sick."

"Well, lookee there." Reva pointed to a chicken-wire cage where two spider monkeys bucked in their breeding. Another lay on a shelf near the roof, stroking himself, awaiting his turn.

"I knowed a woman to mark her baby thataway."

Reva drew her stare away from the monkeys and leveled off scornfully at Carlene's blue eyes.

"Well," Carlene continued bitterly, "my momma told me all about it. Said the gal was nigh onto seven months, an' her husband couldn't drag her away from them monkeys."

Reva looked at the female monkey awaiting her new mount. The other male climbed down for his share as the female's empty face looked back at Reva, blinking.

"That baby was born lookin' just like a monkey," Carlene said, bending herself to talk between Reva and the cage. "Momma swears it's the mark of the beast, but she's real partial to that kinda talk."

"Where is it now?" Reva asked, as if to seek it out.

"Died, I think."

Both males rested, stretched full-length on the floor of the cage, while the female huddled in the corner, glaring. The wind carried their stench away. Now Reva wanted to go to the lockhouse, wanted to feel the chilly floor against her buttocks and shoulders.

The pains in her belly were sharp and familiar. The soreness left her tired and empty. "My stomach hurts," she said to Carlene.

"That sandwich. I tol' ya."

Tyler took her arm, startling her. "We been all to hell an' back tryin' to find ya'll. You look sick," he said, watching a cold pale-ness rise in her cheeks.

"How'd ol' Peepee do?" she asked above the grasp of cramps.

Tyler shook his head.

"Sorry, T.," she said, stroking his cheek. It was already rough.

"You all right?" he asked.

She leaned her face against his chest, letting him hug her. He smelled sweaty and good, but the scent of roe and livestock clung to his skin.

"Yeah, T.," she said, feeling a menstrual slip. She was sorry the rabbit had died for nothing.

⁂

As she went down the steps, Reva did not look for the crushed tunnel of the mole. Instead, she made her way through clouds of gnats toward the river as the moon drove the darkness from the bottom. From deep in the grasses where the snakes were waking up, she saw fireflies speckling the sky and thought she caught scent of something moist in the dry air.

Tyler watched from the porch as his wife passed under the shadows of maples along the riverbank, their foliage making lace of the rising moon across the river. He had lost the prize and the child in the same day, and grew bitter about her spells. "Hey, Jackie," he called, waiting for the tenant to shuffle out to the yard.

"Whut?" The tenant almost screamed from in front of his shack.

"C'mon an' have a drink."

By the moss-softened locks, Reva stared at two moons, one hanging quietly above Ohio, the other broken by the slow current of the river. Mosquitoes buzzed about her ears, taking blood from beneath her tender scalp, but she did not move. Upstream, a deer's hoof sucked in the soft mud, but Reva kept watching the swimming moon — the same moon she knew Clinton watched with his Cincinnati whore. She felt her belly for the child that had never been, and almost wanted the deed undone, even forgotten.

Across the river, a tiny fisherman's-fire danced, and sometimes she thought she could smell its smoke. She stood up, her joints popping from sitting in the dew too long, and traced the carvings in the tree with her cold fingers; felt all that was left of her family: *L.C. N.C. '67.*

Jackie was smiling at the second drink. Tyler made them stronger, laughing at Jackie's stupid grin.

"Whut ya gonna call yer kid?" the tenant asked.

"Ain't gonna be no *kid*," Tyler answered.

"But I's of a mind —"

"You ain't got no mind. Ain't gonna be no *kid*."

Jackie looked stupidly at Tyler. The farmer rubbed his forehead, looking for words.

"She lost her heat," he finally said, hoping Jackie would understand.

They heard a low, simpering whine coming from the porch and went out. Reva sat on the steps, rocking back and forth, hugging herself, whining.

"Goddammit to hell," Tyler said, seeing the orange blades of fire wave out from the lockhouse.

"I done it," Reva said to Jackie, who stood on the step in front of her. She looked up on the porch to her husband. "I done a awful thing, T."

"C'mon, git up'ar," Jackie said, grabbing ner arm to help her up. His huge head hid the moon, and, when she cried against him, the fire. He smelled like coal and whiskey.

❧

THE SCRAPPER

IN the silence between darkness and light, Skeevy awakened, sick from the dream. He rolled over, feeling his head for bumps. There were only a few, but his bones ached from being hit with chairs and his bloody knuckles stuck to the sheets. The shack was dark and hollow as a cistern, and he heard his voice say, "Bund."

The dream had been too real, too much like the real fight with Bund, and he wondered if he had really tried to kill his best friend. His mother begged him to quit boxing when they brought punchy Bund home from the hospital. "Scrap if'n you gotta," she had said, touching the bandage over Skeevy's eye, "but don't you never wear no bandages again. Don't never hurt nobody again."

Trudy mumbled softly in her own dreams, and he slipped from under the covers slowly, trying not to make the springs squeak. He felt empty talking to her, and did not want to be there when she woke up. He dressed and crept to the refrigerator. There was only some rabbit left; still, it was wild meat, and he had to have it.

Outside, a glow from the east was filtering through the fog and turning the ridge pink. Skeevy knew Purserville was across that hill, but he knew the glow could not be from their lights. He started up the western hill toward Clayton wishing he was farther away from Hurricane, from Bund.

As he crested the first knoll, he looked back to the hollow, where he knew Trudy was still sleeping, and far beyond the horizon, where he knew Bund would be sitting on a Coke case in front of the Gulf station begging change, his tongue hanging limp. Skeevy felt his gut skin, and he figured it was just a case of the flux.

At the strip mine, Skeevy sat on a boulder and ate cold rabbit as he looked down on the roofs of Clayton: the company store, company church, company houses, all shiny with fog-wet tin. He saw a miner steal a length of chain from the machine shop where Skeevy worked during the week, promised himself to report it, and forgot it as quickly. Around the houses, he could see where the wives had planted flowers, but the plants were all dead or dying from the constant shower of coal dust.

Just outside of town, across the macadam from the Free Will Church, was The Car, a wheelless dining car left behind after the timber played out. The hulk gleamed like a mussel shell in the Sunday sun.

Skeevy threw his rabbit bones in the brush for the dogs to find, wiped his hands on his jeans, and went down the mountain toward The Car. As he crossed the bottle-cap-strewn pavement of the diner's lot he looked back to where he had sat. The mountain looked like an apple core in the high sun.

Inside, the diner still smelled of sweat and blood from the fight the night before. He shoved the slotted windows open and wondered how ten strong men could find room to fight in The Car. He rubbed his knuckles and smiled. He yawned in the doorway while he waited for the coffee-maker, and through the fog saw Trudy's yellow pantsuit coming down the road.

"Where you been?" he asked.

"You're a'kiddin' me, Skeevy Kelly." She came through the lot smiling, and hooked her arm around him. "You don't show me no respect. Just up an' leave without a good-mornin' kiss."

"I bet you respect real good. I'd respect you till you couldn't walk."

"You're a'kiddin' again. What you want to do today?"

"Bootleg."

"Stop a'kiddin'."

"I ain't, Trudy. I gotta work for Corey," he said, watching her pout.

"Them ol' chicken-fights . . ."

"Well, stick around and talk to Ellen."

"Last time that happened, I ended up smellin' like a hamburger." Skeevy laughed, and she hugged him. "I'll go visit the preacher or somethin'."

"You watch out that 'somethin' ain't about like that," he said, measuring off a length with his arm. She knocked his hand down and started toward the road, until he could only see her yellow slacks pumping through the fog. He liked her, but she made him feel fat and lazy.

"Hey, Trudy," he shouted.

"What?" came from the foggy road.

"Get respected," he said, and heard "I swan to goodness . . ." sigh out of the mist.

A clatter came from the church across the road as two drunken miners dusted themselves down the wooden steps and drifted up the road toward the houses.

Skeevy took two cups from the shelf, filled them, and crossed the road to the church. There was only a shadow of light seeping through the painted window. The old deacon was sweeping bottles from between the pews, talking softly to himself as the glass clanked in empty toasts.

"Here, Cephus." He offered the heavy mug. "Ain't good to start without it."

The skinny old man kept to his chore until the mug grew too heavy for Skeevy and he set it on the pew.

"They had a real brawl," Skeevy offered again.

"Ain't right, drinkin' in a church." The old man looked up

from his work, his brown eyes catching the hazy light. He took up his coffee and leaned on his broom. "How many?" he asked, blowing steam from his brew.

"Even 'nough. 'Bout twenty-five to a side."

"Oooowee," the old man crooned. "Let's get outa here. Lord's abotherin' me for marvelin' at the devil's work."

Once outside, Skeevy noticed how the old man stood straighter, making an effort, grimacing with pain in his back.

"Who won?" Cephus asked.

"Clayton, I reckon. C'mon, I gotta show you a sight."

They crossed the blacktop to the abandoned mill basement beside the diner. There, with its wheels in the air, lay Jim Gibson's pickup truck.

"Five Clayton boys just flipped her in there."

"Damn" was all Cephus could say.

"Nobody in her, but she made one hell of a racket."

"I reckon so." He looked at Skeevy's knuckles.

Skeevy rubbed his hands against his jeans. "Aw, I just tapped a couple when they got bothersome. Those boys fight too serious."

"I usta could," Cephus said, looking back to the murdered truck.

Skeevy looked to the yellow pines on the western hills: the way the light hit them reminded him of grouse-hunting with Bund, of pairing off in the half-day under the woven branches, of the funny human noises the birds made before they flew, and how their necks were always broken when you picked them up.

"You chorin' the juice today?" Cephus kept looking at the truck.

"Sure. Where's the cockfight?"

"I figger they'll meet-up someplace or another," he said, handing Skeevy the cup with " 'Preciate it" as he started for the church. Skeevy side-glanced at the old man to see if his posture drooped, but it did not.

He returned to the diner, plugged in the overplayed jukebox, and threw a few punches at his shadow. He felt tired, and only fried one cheeseburger for breakfast.

Because the woman's back was toward him, Skeevy kept looking at the soft brown scoops of hair. It was clean. Occasionally the man with her would glance at Skeevy to see if he was listening. Being outsiders, they shouted in whispers over their coffee.

Tom and Ellen Corey pulled up in their truck. Ellen's head was thrown back with laughter. Before coming in, they reviewed the upended truck in the neighboring basement. Ellen kept laughing at her short husband as they entered, keeping to the upper side of the counter and away from the customers.

As he leaned over the counter to catch Corey's whispers, Skeevy noticed how Corey's blue eyes were surrounded by white. He had seen the same look in threatened horses.

"Jeb Simpkin's barn," he whispered. "One o'clock."

"Okay."

"Was he all right when he left?" Corey asked.

"Who?"

Skeevy kept his face straight while Ellen sputtered beside him, her hand over her mouth. The outsiders were listening.

"Gibson, dammit. How hard did I lay him?"

"Too hard. You used the club, remember?"

"Oh, shit."

"Yeah," said Skeevy as Ellen broke out laughing.

Skeevy took the keys and went to the Coreys' truck. Across the road, children, women, and old people were shuffling to church. Rev. Jackson and the deacon greeted them at the door, shaking hands. Cephus shot Skeevy a crude salute, and Skeevy made the okay sign as he climbed into the cab. He wondered if Cephus could see it.

As the truck rumbled down the blacktop, Skeevy leaned back

behind the wheel, letting his eyes sag, and he could feel his belly bouncing with the jolts of the truck. He took the revolver from beneath the seat, and watched the roadside for groundhogs to shoot. Between the diner and Corey's coal-dust driveway he saw nothing.

From the cellar of Corey's house he loaded the truck with pint cases of Jack Daniel's and Old Crow: four-dollar bottles that would sell for eight at the cockfight. When he first came to Clayton, he had hated bourbon. He noticed the flies were out, and in Hurricane they would be crawling quietly on Bund's tongue. He opened a case, took a bottle, and drank off half of it. Before the burning stopped, he was at Simpkin's barn, and could hear the chickens screaming.

Warts Hall, a cockfighter from Clayton, came from the barn with a stranger, catching Skeevy as he finished the pint.

"Got any left?" Warts asked. His face was speckled with small cancers.

"More than you can handle," said Skeevy, throwing back the blanket covering the cases. Warts took out two Crows, handing Skeevy a twenty.

"Kindy high, ain't it?" the stranger asked, seeing the change.

"This here's Benny the Punk from Purserville."

"Just a Pursie?" Skeevy asked.

Benny looked as if to lunge.

"Well," Skeevy continued, "I don't put no price on it."

The Punk pretended to read the label on his bottle.

Gibson came out of the barn and Skeevy sidestepped to the cab where the revolver was hidden.

"Got one for me, Skeev?" Gibson asked.

"Sure," Skeevy answered, moving to the truck bed. "I reckon I forgot my cigarettes."

Gibson offered one from his pack and Skeevy took it, handing the man the bottle and pocketing the cash. He noticed the yellow circle around Gibson's eye and temple where the club had met him. Gibson stood drinking as Skeevy counted cases and pretended to be confused.

"Where's the mick?" Gibson asked.

Skeevy turned back smiling. "Ain't got no idy."

"You see him, you tell him I'm alookin'."

"Sure."

The Punk followed Gibson back into the barn, where the game-cocks were crowing.

A wind was rising, pushing the clouds out of the hollow and high over head. Cally, Jeb's daughter, stood on the high front porch of the farmhouse. Skeevy watched her watching him. He had heard Jeb talk of her at work and knew she had been to college in Huntington; he believed Trudy when she said college girls were all looking for rich boys. He watched her clomp down the steps in chunky wooden shoes, and as she crossed the yard between them, he saw how everything from the curve of her hair to the fit of her jeans was too perfect. She looked like the girls he had seen in *Playboy,* and he knew even if she stood beside him, he couldn't have her.

"Your name's Kelly, isn't it?" Her voice was just like the rest of her.

"Yeah," he said, not wanting to say his first name. He knew she would laugh.

"Mom said you were related to Machine Gun Kelly . . ."

He pulled a case out onto the tailgate as if to unload it, wishing somebody had shot the bastard the day he was born.

"He was a cousin of mine — second or third — ever'body's sort of ashamed of him. I don't know nothin' 'bout him."

"I thought you might know something. I'm doing a paper on him for Psych."

"Say what?"

"A paper for Psychology."

Skeevy wondered if she collected maniacs the way men collect gamecocks. He hoisted the case. "Comin' to the main?" he asked. "Gross."

"They don't have to fight if they don't want to," he smiled, carrying the case inside. Seeing Cally standing at the door, he went back for another. She followed him slowly on her chunky shoes.

"Where do you live?" Cally asked.

"In the holler 'twixt Purserville an' Clayton."

She looked puzzled. "But there's nothing there."

"Sure," he said, and wondered if she would add him alongside his cousin in her collection.

They watched as Cephus's truck bounced through the creek and climbed, dripping, up to the barn. Cephus rushed in without speaking, and Skeevy left Cally standing as he followed with another case. When he came out, Corey had her cornered.

"Gibson's lookin' for you," he said to Corey.

"Been talkin' 'bout that very thing to Cally, here —"

"All Mr. Gibson wants is to restore his dignity," she interrupted.

"So I thought we'd arrange a little match. Since you got boxin' in your blood, I'd be willin' to let you stand in. Loser pays for the truck — 'course I'd be willin' to do that, but I know you won't lose."

"I quit boxin' five years ago," Skeevy said, playing with the chain on the tailgate.

"You're quick, boy. I seen you. Don't even have to box. Just dance Gibson to death," Corey laughed. " 'Sides," he said to Cally, "Skeevy loves to scrap."

She giggled.

"Hell, scrappin's different. This here's business."

Cally giggled again.

He looked to the pasture field where wind-pushed clouds were blinking the sun on and off. He spotted a holly tree halfway up the slope. His mother had always liked holly trees. He had never told anybody about his promise to her; he knew they would laugh.

"Two-huntert bucks," he heard himself say.

Corey's eyes grew white rims, but they receded quickly. "Half profit on the booze," he bartered.

"Take it or leave it," Skeevy said, watching Cally smile.

"All right," Corey said. "Cally, you talk good to Jim. Get him to agree on Saturday."

Watching her walk into the barn, Skeevy knew Cally could probably make Jim forget the whole thing. But he was glad for the fight, and began starving for wild meat.

"Where's lunch?" he asked Corey.

In the pit, two light clarets rose in flapping pirouettes. Skeevy neither watched nor bet: newly trained cocks had no form and spent most of their time staying clear of one another.

"Lay off," Cephus yelled. "Ain't no need to make no bird fight. Break for a drink."

For ten minutes, Skeevy and Corey were run ragged handing out bottles and making change. Suddenly there were no more takers, and they still had half a truckload.

"The Pursies ain't buyin' from me after last night," Corey whispered. They loaded all but a half-case into the truck, and Corey took it back to his house.

Leaving the half-case unguarded, Skeevy walked to the pit to examine Warts's bird, a black leghorn with his comb trimmed back to a strawberry. Warts had entered him in the main against a black-breasted red gamer. Skeevy watched as the men fixed two-inch gaffs to the birds' spurs. The Punk stood by him, cleaning his nails with a barlow knife.

"What you want laid up, Benny?"

"Give you eight-to-ten on the red," he said, his knife searching to the quick for a piece of dust.

"Make it," said Skeevy. They placed their money on the ground between them, watching as the two owners touched the birds together, then drew them back eight feet from center.

"Pit!" Cephus yelled, and the cocks strutted toward each other, suddenly meeting in a cloud of feathers.

Warts's rooster backed off, blood gleaming from a gaff mark beneath his right wing.

"Give me —" But before the bettor could finish, the two birds were spurring in midair, then the gamecock lay pinned by the leghorn's gaff.

"Handle!" said the judge, but neither owner moved; they were waiting to hear new odds.

"Dammit, I said 'handle,'" Cephus groaned. The birds were wrung together until they pecked, then set free.

"Even odds," someone shouted. Benny leaned forward for the money, and Skeevy stepped on his hand.

"Get off!"

"Leave it there."

"You heard. It's even."

"You made a bet, Punk. Stick it out or get out."

The Punk left the money.

The birds spun wildly, and again the leghorn came down on the red, his gaff buried in the gamer's back.

"Handle." Cephus was getting bored.

The red's owner, a C&O man from Purserville, poured water on his bird's beak, and blew down its mouth to force air past the clotting blood.

"He's just a Pursie chicken," Skeevy grinned. Benny threw him a cross look.

Warts rubbed his bird to the gamer but got no response.

"Ain't got no fight left," Cephus grumbled.

"Don't quit my bird," the C&O man shouted, his hands and shirt speckled with blood.

110

"If I's as give out as that rooster, I'd need a headstone. Break for a drink."

"Pleasure," Skeevy said to Benny as he picked up his money and returned to the half-case. After selling all but the two bottles in his hip pockets, Skeevy started out the door to look for Cally. Gibson stopped him, smiling.

"I'll make you fight like hell," he warned.

"Well," said Skeevy, "anytime you get to feelin' froggy, just hop on over to your Uncle Skeevy."

"See you Saturday," Gibson laughed.

Outside, he looked for Cally, but she was not around. He went down the farm road, across the blacktop, and up the hills toward his shack. When he topped the first hill, he could see rain coming in from Ohio; and looking back on the tiny people he had left behind, he could see Benny standing with Cally. He wondered if Benny would have to clean his nails again.

Trudy's silence was building as he poured another bourbon and wondered why he gave a good goddamn. When he switched on the light, he disturbed the rest of a hairy winter-fly. He watched it beat against the screen, trying to get to another fly somewhere to breed and die.

"It ain't like I'm boxin' Joe Frazier . . ." He watched her cook and could not recall when she had cared so much about her cooking. "You done tastin' them beans, or you just run outa plates?"

She granted a halted laugh, turned and saw him grinning, and broke into a laughing fit.

"I swan, you made me so mad . . ." she snorted, sitting.

"Ain't nothin' to get mad over."

"Ain't your fight, neither."

"Two-huntert bucks makes it pretty close." He had meant to keep quiet and send the money to Bund. For a moment he saw

111

her eyes open then sag again, and he knew she was worried about the hospital bills. He went back to watching the fly.

Outside the rain fell harder, making petals in the mud. He saw his ghost in the window against the outside's grayness and felt his gut rumble with the flux. Lightly, he touched the scar above his eye, watching as his reflection did the same.

He got up, opened the screen, and let the black fly buzz out into the rain. When he saw the deep holes the drops were making, he wondered if the fly would make it.

"Why don't winter-flies eat?" he asked Trudy.

"I figger they do," she said from the stove.

"Never do," he said, going to the sink to wash.

Taped to the wall was a snapshot of a younger self looking mean over eight-ounce gloves. That was good shape, he thought, fingering the picture. Because it was stained with fat-grease, he left it up.

Trudy put supper down, and they sat.

"You reckon that money would do for a weddin'?" she asked.

"Maybe," he said. "We'll think on it."

They ate.

"Did I ever tell you 'bout the time me an' Bund wrecked the Sunflower Inn?"

"Yeah."

"Oh."

In the stainless steel of the soup machine, Skeevy could see his distorted reflection — real enough to show his features, but not the scar above his eye. His mouth and nose were stuffed with bits of torn rags for padding, and breathing through his mouth made his throat dry.

"Too tight?" Corey asked as he held the bandages wrapped around Skeevy's knuckles. Skeevy shook his head and splayed his fingers to receive the gray muleskin work gloves. He twisted his face to show disgust, and sighed.

"Well, you're the damn boxer," Corey said. "Where's your gloves?"

Skeevy made a zipping motion across his lips and stuck out his right hand to be gloved. He knew it would hurt to get hit with those gloves, but he knew Gibson would hurt more.

A crowd had formed around Corey's truck, and he had Ellen out· there to guard it. She was leaning against the rear fender, talking to a longhair with a camera around his neck. Cally came out of the crowd, put her arm around the longhair, and said something that made Ellen laugh. Skeevy squeezed the gloves tighter around his knuckles.

When Skeevy and Corey came outside the crowd howled with praise and curses; the longhair took a picture of Skeevy, and Skeevy wanted to kill him. They cornered the diner and skidded down the embankment to the newly mown creek-basin. The sun was only a light brown spot in the dusty sky.

Jim Gibson stood naked to the waist, his belly pooching around his belt, his skin so white Skeevy wondered if the man had ever gone shirtless. He grinned at Skeevy, and Skeevy slapped his right fist into his palm and smiled back.

It was nothing like the real fight: Cephus rang a cowbell, Gibson threw one haymaker after another, the entire crowd cursed Skeevy's footwork.

"Quit runnin', chickenshit," someone in the crowd yelled.

In his mind the three minutes were up, but nobody told Cephus to ring the bell. Six minutes, and he knew there would be no bell. Gibson connected to the head. And again. Cheers.

Skeevy tried to go low for the sagging belly, made heavy contact twice, but was disappointed to see the results. He danced some more, dodging haymakers, knowing Gibson could only strike thin air a number of times before weakening. When he saw the time come, he sighted on the man's bruised temple, caught it with a left hook, and dropped him. Then came the bell.

Skeevy felt a stinging in his eye and knew it was blood, but this was nothing like the real fight. This was crazy — Gibson wanted to kill him. Gotta slow him, he thought. Gotta stop him before he kills me.

Cephus rang the bell. Can't believe that goddamned bell, he thought. What the hell is this? Can't see shit. Chest. Wind him. He sighted on the soft concave of Gibson's chest and moved in.

As he threw a right cross to Gibson's chest, Skeevy felt the fine bones of his jaw shatter and tasted blood. Gibson did not fall, and Skeevy danced with the flagging pain. He went again with a combination to the temple. He wanted to tear the eye out and step on it, to feel its pressure building under his foot . . . pop.

As he went down he could hear Trudy screaming his name above the cheers. He lay for a time on the cold floor of the Sunflower Inn: the jukebox played, and he heard Bund coughing. He rolled to his side.

Cephus threw water on Skeevy, and he spat out the bitten-off tip of his tongue. Gibson waited as Skeevy raised himself to a squat. His head cleared, and he knew he could get up.

✹

THE HONORED DEAD

WATCHING little Lundy go back to sleep, I wish I hadn't told her about the Mound Builders to stop her crying, but I didn't know she would see their eyes watching her in the dark. She was crying about a cat run down by a car — her cat, run down a year ago, only today poor Lundy figured it out. Lundy is turned too much like her momma. Ellen never worries because it takes her too long to catch the point of a thing, and Ellen doesn't have any problem sleeping. I think my folks were a little too keen, but Lundy is her momma's girl, not jumpy like my folks.

My grandfather always laid keenness on his Shawnee blood, his half-breed mother, but then he was hep on blood. He even had an oath to stop bleeding, but I don't remember the words. He was a fair to sharp woodsman, and we all tried to slip up on him at one time or another. It was Ray at the sugar mill finally caught him, but he was an old man by then, and his mind wasn't exactly right. Ray just came creeping up behind and laid a hand on his shoulder, and the old bird didn't even turn around; he just wagged his head and said, "That's Ray's hand. He's the first fellow ever slipped up on me." Ray could've done without that, because the old man never played with a full deck again, and we couldn't keep clothes on him before he died.

115

I turn out the lamp, see no eyes in Lundy's room, then it comes to me why she was so scared. Yesterday I told her patches of stories about scalpings and murders, mixed up the Mound Builders with the Shawnee raids, and Lundy chained that with the burial mound in the back pasture. Tomorrow I'll set her straight. The only surefire thing I know about Mound Builders is they must have believed in a God and hereafter or they never would have made such big graves.

I put on my jacket, go into the foggy night, walk toward town. Another hour till dawn, and both lanes of the Pike are empty, so I walk the yellow line running through the valley to Rock Camp. I keep thinking back to the summer me and my buddy Eddie tore that burial mound apart for arrowheads and copper beads gone green with rot. We were getting down to the good stuff, coming up with skulls galore, when of a sudden Grandad showed out of thin air and yelled, "*Wah-pah-nah-te-he.*" He was waving his arms around, and I could see Eddie was about to shit the nest. I knew it was all part of the old man's Injun act, so I stayed put, but Eddie sat down like he was ready to surrender.

Grandad kept on: "*Wah-pah-nah-te-he.* You evil. Make bad medicine here. Now put the goddamned bones back or I'll take a switch to your young asses." He watched us bury the bones, then scratched a picture of a man in the dust, a bow drawn, aimed at a crude sun. "Now go home." He walked across the pasture.

Eddie said, "You Red Eagle. Me Black Hawk." I knew he had bought the game for keeps. By then I couldn't tell Eddie that if Grandad had a shot at the sixty-four-dollar question, he would have sold them on those Injun words: *Wah-pah-nah-te-he* — the fat of my ass.

So I walk and try to be like Ellen and count the pass-at-your-own-risk marks on the road. Eastbound tramples Westbound:

26–17. At home is my own darling Ellen, fast asleep, never knowing who won. Sometimes I wonder if Ellen saw Eddie on his last leave. There are lightning bugs in the fog, and I count them until I figure I'm counting the same ones over. For sure, Lundy would call them Mound Builder eyes, and see them as signals without a message, make up her own message, get scared.

I turn off the Pike onto the oxbow of Front Street, walk past some dark store windows, watch myself moving by their gloss, rippling through one pane and another. I sit on the Old Bank steps, wait for the sun to come over the hills; wait like I waited for the bus to the draft physical, only I'm not holding a bar of soap. I sat and held a bar of soap, wondering if I should shove it under my arm to hike my blood pressure into the 4-F range. My blood pressure was already high, but the bar of soap would give me an edge. I look around at Front Street and picture people and places I haven't thought of in years; I wonder if it was that way for Eddie.

I put out my hand like the bar of soap was in it and see its whiteness reflect blue from the streetlights long ago. And I remember Eddie's hand flattened on green felt, arched knuckles cradling the cue for a tough eight-ball shot, or I remember the way his hand curled around his pencil to hide answers on math tests. I remember his hand holding an arrowhead or unscrewing a lug nut, but I can't remember his face.

It was years ago, on Decoration Day, and my father and several other men wore their Ike jackets, and I was in the band. We marched through town to the cemetery in the rain; then I watched the men move sure and stiff with each command, and the timing between volleys was on the nose; the echoes rang four times above the clatter of their bolt weapons. The rain smelled from the tang of their fire, the wet wool of our uniforms. There was a pause and the band director coughed. I stepped up to play, a little off tempo, and another kid across the hills answered my taps. I finished first, snapped my bugle back. When the last tone seeped through to mist, it beat at me, and I could swear I heard the stumps of Eddie's arms beating the coffin lid for us to stop.

I look down at my hand holding the bugle, the bar of soap. I look at my hand, empty, older, tell myself there is no bar of soap in that hand. I count all five fingers with the other hand, tell myself they are going to stay there a hell of a long time. I get out a cigarette and smoke. Out on the Pike, the first car races by in the darkness, knowing no cops are out yet. I think of Eddie pouring on the gas, heading with me down the Pike toward Tin Bridge.

That day was bright, but the blink of all the dome lights showed up far ahead of us. We couldn't keep still for the excitement, couldn't wait to see what happened.

I said, "Did you hear it, man? I thought they'd dropped the Bomb."

"Hear? I felt it. The damn ground shook."

"They won't forget that much noise for a long time."

"For sure."

Cars were stopped dead-center of the road, and a crowd had built up. Eddie pulled off to the side behind a patrol car, then made his way through the crowd, holding his wallet high to show his volunteer fireman's badge. I kept back, but in the break the cops made, I saw the fire was already out, and all that was left of Beck Fuller's Chevy was the grille, the rest of the metal peeled around it from behind. I knew it was Beck's from the '51 grille, and I knew what had happened. Beck fished with dynamite and primer cord, and he was a real sport to the end. Beck could never get into his head he had to keep the cord away from the TNT.

Then a trooper yelled: "All right, make way for the wrecker."

Eddie and the other firemen put pieces of Beck the Sport into bags, and I turned away to keep from barfing, but the smell of burning hair drifted out to me. I knew it was the stuffing in old car-seats, and not Beck, but I leaned against the patrol car, tossed my cookies just the same. I wanted to stop being sick because it was silly to be sick about something like that. Under the noise of my coughings I could hear the fire chief cussing Eddie into just getting the big pieces, just letting the rest go.

Eddie didn't sit here with any bar of soap in his hand. He never had much gray matter, but he made up for it with style, so he would never sit here with any bar of soap in his hand. Eddie would never think about blowing toes away or cutting off his trigger finger. It just was not his way to think. Eddie was the kind who bought into a game early, and when the deal soured, he'd rather hold the hand a hundred years than fold. It was just his way of doing.

At Eight Ball, I chalked up while Eddie broke. The pool balls cracked, but nothing went in, and I moved around the table to pick the choice shot. "It's crazy to join," I said.

"What the hell — I know how to weld. They'll put me in welding school and I'll sit it out in Norfolk."

"With your luck the ship'll fall on you."

"Come on, Eagle, go in buddies with me."

"Me and Ellen's got plans. I'll take a chance with the lottery." I shot, and three went in.

"That's slop," Eddie said.

I ran the other four down, banked the eight ball to a side pocket, and stood back, made myself grin at him. The eight went where I called it, but I never believed I made the shot right, and I didn't look at Eddie, I just grinned.

I toss my cigarette into the gutter, and it glows back orange under the blue streetlight. I think how that glow would be just another eye for Lundy, and think that after a while she will see so many eyes in the night they won't matter anymore. The eyes will go away and never come back, and even if I tell her when she is grown, she won't remember. By then real eyes will scare her enough. She's Ellen's girl, and sometimes I want to ask Ellen if she saw Eddie on his last leave.

Time ago I stood with my father in the cool evening shadow of the barn to smoke; he stooped, picked up a handful of gravel, and flipped them away with his thumb. He studied on what I said about Canada, and each gravel falling was a little click in his thoughts; then he stood, dusted his palms. "I didn't mind it too much," he said. "Me and Howard kept pretty thick in foxhole religion — never thought of running off."

"But, Dad, when I seen Eddie in that plastic bag . . ."

He yelled: "Why the hell'd you look? If you can't take it, you oughtn't to look. You think I ain't seen that? That and worse, by god."

I rub my hand across my face, hang my arm tight against the back of my neck, think I ought to be home asleep with Ellen. I think, if I was asleep with Ellen, I wouldn't care who won. I wouldn't count or want to know what the signals mean, and I wouldn't be like some dog looking for something dead to drag in.

When Eddie was in boot camp, me and Ellen sat naked in the loft at midnight, scratching fleas and the itch of hay. She went snooping through a box of old books and papers, and pulled out a bundle of letters tied with sea-grass string. Her flashlight beamed over my eyes as she stepped back to me, and watching her walk in the color tracings the light left in my eyes, I knew she would be my wife. She tossed the package in my lap, and I saw the old V-mail envelopes of my father's war letters. Ellen lay flat on her back, rested her head on my thigh, and I took up the flashlight to read.

"*Dear folks. We are in* — the name's been cut out."

"Why?" She rolled to her stomach, looked up at me.

I shrugged. "I guess he didn't know he couldn't say that. *The way they do thes people is awful bad. I found a rusky prisoner starven in the street and took him to a german house for a feed.*" I felt Ellen's tongue on the inside of my thigh and shivered, tried to keep reading. "*They didn't do nothin for him till I leveled off with my gun and Howard he raised hell with me only I seen that rusky eat one damn fine meal.*" I turned off the flashlight, moved down beside Ellen. He had never told that story.

But it's not so simple now as then, not easy to be a part of Ellen without knowing or wanting to know the web our kisses make. It was easy to leave the house with a bar of soap in my pocket; only the hardest part was sitting here, looking at it, and remembering.

I went through the hall with the rest of the kids between classes, and there stood Eddie at the top of the stairs. He grinned at me, but it was not his face anymore. His face had changed; a face gone red because the other kids snickered at his uniform. He stood at parade rest, his seaman's cap hanging from his belt, his head tilting back to look down on me, then he dragged his hands around like Jackie Gleason taking an away-we-go pool shot. We moved on down the hall to ditch my books.

"You on leave?" I said.

"Heap bad medicine. Means I'm getting shipped."

"How long?" I fumbled with the combination of my locker.

"Ten days," he said, then squinted at the little upside-down flag on my open locker door. "You sucker."

I watched him until he went out of sight down the steps, then got my books, went on to class.

The butt of my palm is speckled with black spots deep under the skin: cinders from a relay-race fall. The skin has sealed them over, and it would cost plenty to get them out. Sometimes Ellen wants to play nurse with a needle, wants to pry them out, but I won't let her. Sometimes I want to ask Ellen if she saw Eddie on his last leave.

Coach said I couldn't run track because anyone not behind his country was not fit for a team, so I sat under the covered bridge waiting for the time I could go home. Every car passing over sprinkled a little dust between the boards, sifted it into my hair.

I watched the narrow river roll by, its waters slow but muddy like pictures I had seen of rivers on the TV news. In history class, Coach said the Confederate troops attacked this bridge, took it, but were held by a handful of Sherman's troops on Company Hill. Johnny Reb drank from this river. The handful had a spring on Company Hill. Johnny croaked with the typhoid and the Yankees moved south. So I stood and brushed the dust off me. My hair grew long after Eddie went over, and I washed it every night.

I put my fist under my arm like the bar of soap and watch the veins on the back of my hand rise with pressure. There are scars where I've barked the hide hooking the disk or the drag to my tractor; they are like my father's scars.

We walked the fields, checked the young cane for blight or bugs, and the late sun gave my father's slick hair a sparkle. He chewed the stem of his pipe, then stood with one leg across a knee and banged tobacco out against his shoe.

I worked up the guts: "You reckon I could go to college, Dad?"

"What's wrong with farming?"

"Well, sir, nothing, if that's all you ever want."

He crossed the cane rows to get me, and my left went up to guard like Eddie taught me, right kept low and to the body.

"Cute," he said. "Real cute. When's your number up?"

I dropped my guard. "When I graduate — it's the only chance I got to stay out."

He loaded his pipe, turned around in his tracks like he was looking for something, then stopped, facing the hills. "It's your damn name is what it is. Dad said when you was born, 'Call him William Haywood, and if he ever goes in a mine, I hope he chokes to death.' "

I thought that was a shitty thing for Grandad to do, but I watched Dad, hoped he'd let me go.

He started up: "Everybody's going to school to be something better. Well, when everybody's going this way, it's time to turn around and go that way, you know?" He motioned with his hands in two directions. "I don't care if they end up shitting gold nuggets, somebody's got to dig in the damn ground. Somebody's got to."

And I said, "Yessir."

The sky is dark blue and the fog is cold smoke staying low to the ground. In this first hint of light my hand seems blue, but not cold; such gets cold sooner or later, but for now my hand is warm.

Many's the time my grandfather told of the last strike before he quit the mines, moved to the valley for some peace. He would quit his Injun act when he told it, like it was real again, all before him, and pretty soon I started thinking it was *me* the Baldwin bulls were after. *I* ran through the woods till my lungs bled. *I* could hear the Baldwins and their dogs in the dark woods, and *I* could remember machine guns cutting down pickets, and all *I* could think was how the One Big Union was down the rathole. Then I could taste it in my mouth, taste the blood coming up from my lungs, feel the bark of a tree root where I fell, where I slept. When I opened my eyes, I felt funny in the gut, felt watched. There were no twig snaps, just the feeling that something was too close. Knowing it was a man, one man, hunting me, I took up my revolver. I could hear him breathing, aimed into the sound, knowing the only sight would come with the flash. I knew all my life I had lived to kill this man, this goddamned Baldwin man, and I couldn't do it. I heard him move away down the ridge, hunting his lost game.

I fold my arms tight like I did the morning the bus pulled up. I was thinking of my grandfather, and there was a bar of soap under my arm. At the draft physical, my blood pressure was clear out of sight, and they kept me four days. The pressure never went down, and on the fourth day a letter came by forward. I read it on the bus home.

Eddie said he was with a bunch of Jarheads in the Crotch, and he repaired radio gear in the field. He said the USMC's hated him because he was regular Navy. He said the chow was rotten, the quarters lousy, and the left side of his chest was turning yellow from holding smokes inside his shirt at night. And he said he knew how the guy felt when David sent him into the battle to get dibs on the guy's wife. Eddie said he wanted dibs on Ellen, ha, ha. He said he would get married and give me his wife if I would get him out of there. He said the beer came in Schlitz cans, but he was sure it was something else. Eddie was sure the CO was a fag. He said he would like to get Ellen naked, but if he stayed with this outfit he would want to get me naked when he came back. He asked if I remembered him teaching me to burn off leeches with a cigarette. Eddie swore he learned that in a movie where the hero dies because he ran out of cigarettes. He said he had plenty of cigarettes. He said he could never go Oriental because they don't have any hair on their twats, and he bet me he knew what color Ellen's bush was. He said her hair might be brown, but her bush was red. He said to think about it and say Hi to Ellen for him until he came back. Sometimes I want to ask Ellen if she saw Eddie on his last leave.

When I came back, Ellen met me at the trailer door, hugged me, and started to cry. She showed pretty well with Lundy, and I told her Eddie's letter said to say Hi. She cried some more, and I knew Eddie was not coming back.

Daylight fires the ridges green, shifts the colors of the fog, touches the brick streets of Rock Camp with a reddish tone. The streetlights flicker out, and the traffic signal at the far end of Front Street's yoke snaps on; stopping nothing, warning nothing, rushing nothing on.

I stand and my joints crack from sitting too long, but the flesh of my face is warming in the early sun. I climb the steps of the Old Bank, draw a spook in the window soap. I tell myself that spook is Eddie's, and I wipe it off with my sleeve, then I see the bus coming down the Pike, tearing the morning, and I start down the street so he won't stop for me. I cannot go away, and I cannot make Eddie go away, so I go home. And walking down the street as the bus goes by, I bet myself a million that my Lundy is up and already watching cartoons, and I bet I know who won.

THE WAY IT HAS TO BE

ALENA stepped under the awning of the Tastee Freeze and looked out at the rain draining into the dust, splattering craters with little clouds. When it stopped, cars hissed along the highway in whorls of mist. She stood by the slotted window, peering through the dirty glass to empty freezers and sills speckled with the crisp skeletons of flies. Far down the parking lot stood a phone booth, but as she stirred circles in the bottle caps and gravel, she knew she could not call home.

She sat on a lip of step by the porcelain drinking fountain and watched Harvey's head lolling against the car window, his holster straps arching slack above his shoulders. She felt her stomach twitch, and tried to rub her eyes without smearing. She didn't want it this way, but knew Harvey would never change. She laughed a little; she had only come from West Virginia to see the cowboys, but all this range was farmed and fenced. The openness freed and frightened her.

Harvey jostled, rolled down the window. There was a white dust of drool on his chin. "Wanna drive?" he said.

She started toward the car. "All last night I worried. Momma's cannin' stuff today."

"Lay off," he said. "You gotta right to get out." He tightened his holster and pulled on his jacket.

"You love that thing?"

"He's got it comin'."

"Parole catches you, you got lots more."

"Lay off, it's too early," he said, reaching for a cigarette.

While she drove, Alena saw the haze lift, but not like a dew. Instead, it left a dust film and far ahead there was always more haze. As they skirted Oklahoma City, it thickened, and the heat stuck to their skin. She pulled off at a hamburger stand and Harvey got out while she looked at the map. In a side panel, a picture of the Cowboy Hall of Fame called her away from the route. Harvey came back with a bag of sandwiches and coffee.

"Harv, let's go here," she said, offering the picture.

He looked, then grabbed her thigh just below the crotch and kissed her. "There'll be plenty of time after this."

As they ate, Harvey took a slip of paper from his shirt pocket and checked the map. He stared at the dashboard for a long time, thinking. Alena watched his brow draw tight, but she could not ask him to give it up. She hoped Harvey was not dumb enough to kill him.

Harvey took the wheel and they drove down a small secondary toward a farm. Alena watched the land slip by, growing flatter, longer in the new heat. Always the steady haze hid the horizon, and she wished she would see a cowboy.

The stairwell was empty, quiet, yet Alena's nerves twisted again as she looked at Harvey. He walked uneasily and his eyes were crossed from the whiskey. Two flights up and they opened their door. The room was small and old-fashioned, and opened to the street, where the dust storm turned the streetlights yellow. Harvey took off his jacket, opened his satchel and got out the whiskey. He was shaking, and his gun flapped loosely in its holster.

"Jesus, Harvey," she said, sitting on the bed.

"Will you shut up?"

She could still see it: the man reached out to shake and Harvey handed him three in the chest. "I'm afraid," she said, and could not forget the old woman sitting on the porch, stringing beans. Alena wondered if she still sat there, her mouth open, her son dead in the yard.

"Have a drink," Harvey said. He had stopped shaking.

"I'm gonna barf."

"Barf then, dammit." He rubbed his neck hard.

She stood by the sink and looked into the drain, but nothing would come up. "What're we gonna do?"

"Stay here," he said, finishing the pint, looking for another.

"I'm sorry I'm scared," she said, and turned on the water to wash her face.

"Lay down," Harvey said, standing by the window.

Alena sat in the chair by the sink, watching Harvey. His pint half gone, he leaned against the window casement. Not the man she knew in the hills, he looked skinny and meaner to her, and now she knew he was a murderer, that the gun he always carried had worked. She was not part of him now; it was over so easily she wondered if they had ever loved.

"We'll go to Mexico and get married," he said.

"I can't, I'm too scared."

Harvey turned toward her, the yellow light of the street glowing against his face and chest.

"The whole time I was in," he said, "I waited for two things: to kill him, and to marry you."

"I can't, Harvey. I didn't know."

"What? That I love you?"

"No, the other. I thought it was talk."

"I don't talk," he said, and took a drink.

"God, I wish you hadn't."

"Whadaya want? To be back in the hills?"

"Yes, I don't want this anymore. I hate this."

He pulled his gun and pointed it at her. She sat, looking at him, his eyes wide with fear, and she leaned over the chair and threw up a stream of yellow bile. When she stopped coughing and wiped her chin, Harvey sat slumped in the corner, the pistol dangling in his hand.

"You goddamned bitch," he muttered. "Now I need you and you're a goddamned bitch." He lifted the pistol to his temple, but Alena saw him smile. A puff of air came from his lips, and he put the gun in its holster.

"I'm gonna get drunk," he said, standing up. "You suit yourself. I'm not comin' back." Down the hall, she could hear him bumping against the walls.

Alena washed herself, then turned on the light. Her eyes were circled and red, her lips chapped. She put on makeup and went out.

As she walked down the street, the dust blew papers against her ankles, and she went into a café with a Help Wanted sign. The girl behind the counter looked bored when Alena ordered a beer.

"You need help?"

"Not now, only in the morning. Come in the morning and ask for Pete. He'll probably put you on."

"Thanks," she said, and sipped.

In the back was a phone booth, and Alena carried her beer to it. She made the call, and the phone rang twice.

"Hello, Momma."

"Alena," her voice trembled.

"I'm in Texas, Momma. I come with Harvey."

"Stringin' round with trash. We spoiled you rotten, that's what we done."

"I just didn't want you all to worry."

There was a long quiet. "Come on back, Alena."

"I can't, Momma. I got a job. Ain't that great?"

"Top shelf in the cupboard fell down and made a awful mess. I been worried it's a token."

"No, Momma, it's all right, you hear? I got a job."

"All that jelly we put up is busted."

"It's all right, Momma, you got a bunch left."

"I reckon."

"I gotta go, Momma. I love you."

The phone clicked.

The night calmed, and most of the dust settled in eddies by the curb. As she walked along to the hotel, Alena felt better. Harvey was gone, but it didn't matter. She had a job, and she was in Texas.

As she passed through the lobby of the hotel, the clerk smiled at her, and she liked it. But on the landing to the room, Harvey waited. Cigarette butts were all around his feet, and he was rumpled, cripple-looking.

"I come back to apologize," he said, standing to hold her. She fell against him.

"Nothin's changed," she said. "I'm stayin' here."

"That's it?"

She nodded. "I got a job, so I called home. Everything's okay."

"Can we talk upstairs?"

"Sure," she said.

"Then let's talk," and his hand brushed against the revolver as he reached for another cigarette.

＊

THE SALVATION OF ME

C HESTER was smarter than any shithouse mouse because
Chester got out before the shit began to fall. But Chester had
two problems: number one, he became a success, and number
two, he came back. These are not your average American problems like drinking, doping, fucking, or being fucked, because Rock
Camp, West Virginia, is not your average American problem maker,
nor is it your average hillbilly town.

You have never broken a mirror or walked under ladders or
celebrated Saint Paddy's day if you have never heard of Rock
Camp, but you might have lost a wheel, fallen off a biplane wing,
or crossed yourself left-handedly if you have. The three latter
methods are the best ways to get into Rock Camp, and any viable
escape is unknown to anybody but Chester, and he is unavailable
for comment.

It was while Archie Moore — the governor, not the fighter —
was in his heyday that the sweet tit of the yellow rose of Texas ran
dry, forcing millions of Americans down to the survival speed of
55 mph. I have heard it said that Georgians are unable to drive
in snow, and that Arizonans go bonkers behind the wheel in the
rain, but no true-blooded West Virginia boy would ever do less
than 120 mph on a straight stretch, because those runs are hard
won in a land where road maps resemble a barrel of worms with
Saint Vitus' dance. It was during this time that Chester discov-

ered people beating it through West Virginia via Interstate 64 on their way to more interesting places like Ohio and Iowa, and for the first time in his life Chester found fourth gear in his Chevy with the Pontiac engine. Don't ask me what the transmission was, because I was sick the day they put it in and don't ask me where Chester went, because I didn't see him again for four years, and then he wasn't talking.

All I know for sure is that Chester made it big, and came back to show it off, and that I never hated him more in the years he was gone than I did the two hours he was home. The fact that without Chester I had twice as many cars to fix, half as much gas to pump, and nobody to road-race or play chicken with on weekends made up for itself in giving me all my own cigarettes, since Chester was the only bum in the station. And his leaving warmed over an old dream.

Back in '61 when I was a school kid, everybody from one end of Rock Camp to the other switched over from radio to TV, and although I still believe that was a vote purchase on Kennedy's part, everyone swears it was a benefit of working in the pre–Great Society days. So the old Hallicrafters radio found its place next to my desk and bed, looking at me, as it later did through hours of biology homework, like any minute the Day of Infamy would come out of its speakers again.

What did come out, and only between the dusk and dawn, was WLS from Chicago. Chicago became a dream, then more of a habit than pubescent self-abuse, replaced beating off, then finally did what the health teacher said pounding the pud would do — made me crazy as a damn loon.

Chicago, Chicago, that toddlin' town . . .

Don't ask me to sing the rest, because I have forgotten it, and don't ask me what became of the dream, either, because I have a sneaking suspicion Chester did it in for me when he came back. But the dream was more beautiful than the one about Mrs. Dent, my sex-goddess math teacher, raping hell out of me during a tutoring session, and the dream was more fun because I believed it could happen. When I asked Mr. Dent, the gym teacher, if the angle of his dangle was equal to the heat of her meat, he rammed my head into a locker, and I swore forever to keep my hand out of my Fruit of the Looms. Besides, Chicago had it over Mrs. Dent by a mile, and Chicago had more Mrs. Dents than could rape me in a million years.

Dex Card, the then–night jock for 'LS, had a Batman fan club that even I could belong to, and the kids in Chicago all had cars, wore h.i.s. slacks — baked by the friendly h.i.s. baker in his own little oven so the crease would never wash out. They all chewed Wrigley gum, and all went to the Wrigley Building, which for some reason seems, even today, like a giant pack of Juicy Fruit on end. The kids in Chicago were so close to Motown they could drive up and *see* Gladys Knight or the Supremes walking on the goddamned street. And the kids in Chicago had three different temperatures: if it was cold at O'Hare Airport, it was colder in the Loop, and it was always below zero on the El. It took me ten years to get the joke. It took us two days to get the weather — if it rained in Chicago on Monday, I wore a raincoat on Wednesday, and thought of it as Chicago rain.

After the dream came the habit. I decided to run off to Chicago, but hadn't figured what I could do to stay alive, and I didn't know Soul One in the town. But the guys on 'LS radio sounded like decent sorts, and they had a real warmth you could just hear when they did those Save the Children ads. You knew those guys would be the kind to give a poor kid a break. And that is where the habit and the dream got all mixed up.

I would maybe take the train — since that was the only way I knew to get out, from my father's Depression stories — and I might even meet A-Number-One on some hard-luck flatcar, and him tracing old dreams on the car floor with a burned-out cigarette.

Then me and old A-Number-One would take the Rock Island out of Kentucky, riding nonstop coal into the Chicago yards, and A-Number-One would tell about whole trains getting swallowed up, lost, bums and all, in the vastness of everything, never found. But I would make it off the car before she beat into the yards, skirt the stink on that side, and there I was at the Loop.

I would find WLS Studios and ask for a job application, and the receptionist, sexier than Mrs. Dent and a single to boot, would ask me what I could do. I would be dirty from the train, and my clothes would not be h.i.s., so what could I say but that I would like to sweep up. Bingo, and they hire me because nobody in Chicago ever wants to sweep up, and when I get down to scrape the Wrigley's off the floor, they think I'm the best worker in the world. I figure I'd better mop, and Dex Card says I'm too smart to mop and for me to take this sawbuck, go buy me some h.i.s. clothes and show up here tomorrow. He says he wants me to be the day jock, and he will teach me to run the board, make echoes, spin the hits, double-up the sound effects, and switch to the news-weather-and-sports. Hot damn.

So I sat at the desk every night, learning less biology, dreaming the dream over and over, until one night I looked at my respectable — nevertheless Woolworth — slacks, and realized that the freight trains no longer slowed down at Rock Camp. There was always the bus, but in all three times I collected enough pop bottles for a ticket to where the train slowed down, the pool balls would break in my ears, and quarters would slip away into slots of time and chance.

"You can't see the angles," Chester said to me one day after he ran the table in less than a minute.

I was in the tenth grade and didn't give two shits for his advice. All I knew was all my quarters were gone, there were no more pop bottles along the Pike, and Chicago was still a thousand miles away. I just leaned on my stick: I was sheared and I knew it.

136

"You know anything about cars?" I shook my head no. "Can you work a gas pump?" Again no. "You *can* wash a car." I sneered a who-the-hell-couldn't.

And from that day I went to work for E. B. "Pop" Sullivan in his American Oil station at seventy-five cents an hour, one-third of which went to Chester for getting me the job. I told myself it didn't matter, I wasn't going to make a career of it, I was hitting it for Chicago as soon as I got the money — I'd ride the buses all the way, I'd drive. What the hell, I'd save up and buy a car to take me to Chicago in style.

When I told Chester I wanted to buy a car, he let me off the hook for his fee, even took me to look at the traps on the car lot. Then I told Chester I didn't want a trap, I wanted a real car.

"That's the way you get a real one," he said. "You make it to suit yourself — Motown just makes them to break down."

We looked at a Pontiac with only 38,000 and a 327. Somebody had lamed in the rear and pushed the trunk into the back seat. There was a clump of hair hanging from the chrome piece around the window. Chester crawled under this car and was gone for almost five minutes, while I was more attracted to a Chevy Impala with a new paint job and a backyard, install-it-yourself convertible top that came down of its own when you pressed a button. Chester came out from under the Pontiac like he had found a snake, then walked over to me grinning.

"She's totaled to hell and back, but the engine's perfect."

I told Chester I liked the Impala, but he just sucked his teeth like he knew what happened to tops that come down of their own. He walked all around the car, bent over to look under it, rubbed his fingers along the tread of the tires, and all the time I kept staring at the $325 soaped on the windshield. Sure, the Pontiac was cheaper, but who wanted to pay $130 to walk around with an engine under his arm? Not me, I wanted to drive it away, make the top go up and down.

"Tell you what," he said. "I got me a nice Chevy for that Pontiac's motor. You buy the motor — I'll rent the body to you."

I wasn't about to bite, so I shook my head.

"We'll be partners, then. We'll each only sell out to the other, and we'll stick together on weekends. You know, double dates."

That made a little more sense, and the rest of that month the Chicago dream went humming away to hide someplace in my brain. I had nightmares about adapters being stretched out to fit an engine that shouldn't be in a Chevy. I worried about tapping too far from the solid part of the block, could just see cast steel splintering the first time we forced her up to 80. I went to drag races, asked anybody I saw if you could put a Pony engine in a Chevy, and most people laughed, but one smart-ass leaned back in his chair: "Son," says the smart-ass, "go play with yourself."

But the month went by, and the engine, for some reason I never understood, went in, but all the fire wall and all the fender wells came out. When Chester came down to the transmission problem, I came down with the flu, and for three days I neither dreamed of Chicago nor my car because I was too busy being sick. On returning to school, I saw her in the parking lot, the rear end jacked up with shackles, and when I looked in on the gearshift, Chester had a four-speed pattern knob screwed on it. I thought it was a joke, because I never saw the last gear used. She did 50 wound tight in third, and that was enough for the straight piece in the Pike.

That summer was just one big time. Chester and I spent every cent we earned on gas and every free minute on the back roads. We discovered a bridge with enough hump that hitting it at 45 would send us airborne every time and make the buggy rock like a chair until we could get new shocks on it. Unbeknownst to him, Pop Sullivan supplied shocks all summer. We found a curved section of one-lane that was almost always good for a near head-on with a Pepsi truck. A couple of times, Pop supplied red-lead to disguise the fact that we had gotten too close to the Pepsi truck. Pepsi, I take it, got the message and rerouted the driver. Chester told me, "They sent a boy to do a man's job."

But the best fun came when a Cabell County deputy was on his way to summons some ridge runner to court for not sharing his liquor revenues with the state. Deputy met us coming downhill and around a curve at top speed, and there was little else for Deputy to do but give us the right-of-way or kiss all our sweet asses good-bye. Deputy was a very wise man. Figuring that anybody coming from nowhere that fast had something to hide, Deputy then radioed ahead the liquor was in our car. They nabbed us at the foot of the hill, stone-cold sober, and found us holding no booze at all. What they did find were Deputy's two daughters — both out with their momma's permission. Chester got three days for driving away from a deputy, and neither of us was allowed to call the girls again. Don't ask me what their momma got, as I am not sure if Deputy was the wife-beating kind or not.

Chester served his three days in Sundays reading the paper at the county jail, and the first Sunday changed him considerably for the worse. At work the next day he wouldn't talk about who he wanted to go out with or where we were going to find money for the next tankful, but by the weekend he loosened up. "It's all a matter of chance," he said. I thought he was trying to explain his jail sentence. It took four years before I figured it out. After his second Sunday, he came back with a sneak in his eyes like he was just waiting for something to drop on his back out of thin air. "It's out there for sure, but it's just a matter of being in the right place when the shit falls." I agreed all the way. It was all in Chicago, and school was starting and I was still in Rock Camp.

The next morning, Chester went on the lam in a most interesting manner. It was his turn to cruise around town in the car during lunch, smooching his woman, and I would get snatch for my grab on the high-school steps. We had both been caught getting too fresh with our girls, and now there was not a decent girl in Rock Camp that wouldn't claim one of us raped her after her football boyfriend knocked her up. So it was that Chester's main squeeze was a girl from Little Tokyo Hollow, where twice-is-nice-but-incest-is-best and all the kids look like gooks. So it was I had no woman that day. And Chester was making the main circuit with regular rounds so that from where I sat, I could see every move this slant-eye made.

The first three go-arounds were pretty standard, and I could almost measure the distance her hand had moved on the way to Chester's crotch, but on the fourth trip she had him wide and was working the mojo. I knew Chester had done some slick bargaining to get that much action that soon, and I figured it was over from there, since I saw him turn around and head west back to the school. He was still only cruising, taking his time like he knew the bell would never ring unless he had gone to his locker. Then on the way by, I saw the slant-eye going down on him, her head bobbing like mad, Chester smiling, goosing the gas in short spurts. It wasn't until he stopped at the town limits and put the girl out that I figured Chester didn't care about coming back to class, but I went on anyway, sure as I could be that he'd be back tomorrow.

That afternoon the guidance counselor called me in and asked me what I was doing with the rest of my life. It seemed Chester's slant-eye had spilled the beans, and they were thinking there was something in me they could save. I told the guidance counselor I wanted to work for a radio station in Chicago — just as a joke.

"Well, you'll have to go to college for that, you know."

It was news to me, because Dex Card didn't sound like a teacher or a doctor, and I said no.

That evening, when Chester didn't show for work, I asked Pop Sullivan to sponsor me through college. I promised to stay at the station until I got my journalism degree, then send him the difference.

"I got all the difference I need" was all Pop would say. He kept looking out the window for Chester to come fix his share of cars. Chester never came, so I stayed until the next morning and figured out how to fix both our shares of cars with a book, and I thought maybe that was the way Chester had done it all along.

A week later, Pop hired another kid to pump gas and raised me to minimum wage, which by Archie's heyday was about a buck fifty. That was when I got a telegram from Cleveland saying: "Sorry Pard, I got it into fourth and couldn't get it out. I'll make it up sometime, C." — and I wondered why Chester bothered to waste four cents on the "Pard."

I left the radio off and my grades went up a little, but I didn't think I'd learned much worth knowing. The guidance counselor kept this shit-eating grin for when she passed me in the hall. Then weird stuff started happening — like my old man would come to bed sober at night and go to church twice on Sunday and drink orange juice at breakfast without pitching a bitch at me. And I got invited to parties the football players' parents threw for them and their girls, but I never went. Then a teacher told me if I made a B in World History before Christmas I would be a cinch for the Honor Society, but I told that teacher in no uncertain terms what the Honor Society could go do with themselves, and the teacher said I was a smart-ass. I agreed. I still got the B. I started dating Deputy's youngest daughter again, and he acted like I was a quarterback.

Then the real shit came down. It was snowing tons before Christmas, so I cut school to help Pop clear the passage around the pumps, and he called the principal to tell him what was up. I was salting the sidewalks when Pop yelled at me to come inside, then he loaded his pipe and sat down behind the desk.

"What'd I tell you about stealing?" he says, but I set him

straight that I wasn't holding anything of his. "I don't mean you are, only I want to know if you remember." I told him that he had said once-a-thief-always-a-thief about a million times. "Do you think that's so?" I asked him if he'd stolen before. "Just once, but I put it back." I told him once-a-thief-always-a-thief, but he just laughed. "You need a college sponsor. I need another Catholic in this town." I assured Pop that my old man had suddenly seen the light, but I was in no way, shape, or form walking his path with him, and he was Methodist to boot. "You think about it." I said I would think about it and went in to grease a car. All I could think was, Dex Card doesn't sound like a Catholic name.

I walked home in the snow that night, and it did not seem like Chicago snow — it seemed like I was a kid before the radio moved into my room, and like when I got home from sledding and my old lady was still alive, still pumping coffee into me to cut the chill, and I missed her just a little.

I went inside hoping my old man would have a beer in his hand just so I could put things back to normal again, but he was sitting in the kitchen reading a newspaper, and he was stoned sober out of his mind.

I fixed us some supper, and while we ate he asked me if Pop had said anything to me about college. I said he would sponsor me if I turned mackerel-snapper. "Not a bad deal. You going to take it?" I assured him I was thinking on it. "There's mail for you," and he handed me an envelope postmarked Des Moines, Iowa. Inside was seventy-five bucks and a scrap of paper that said: "Less depreciation. *Adios*, C." I put the money in my wallet and balled up the note. "You can buy some clothes with that wad," he said. I assured my old man that I would need a car more if I was to drive to college every day, but he just laughed, gave me a dutch rub from across the table. He told me I was a good kid for a punk. Even the women in the school cafeteria sent me a card saying I was bound to become a man of letters — on the inside was a cartoon mailman. It took me a while to get the joke.

And about that time the price of gas went up. I bought a '58 VW without a floor, drove it that way until it rained, then bought a floor for more than I paid for the whole car. Deputy's daughter missed a couple of months and decided it was me, and it probably was, so she joined me in catechism and classes at the community college in Huntington, and we lived in a three-room above Pop's station. The minute Deputy's daughter lost the kid, Deputy had the whole thing annulled, and Pop made me move back in with my old man. My old man started drinking again. I quit school, but stayed on at Pop Sullivan's garage to pay him back, and it was about then that I saw the time had gone by too soon. I had not turned the old radio on in all these years and I couldn't stand to now. I decided working for Pop wasn't too bad, and pretty soon my old man was going to have to be put away, and I'd need the money for that.

I drove home in the VW singing, "*Chicago, Chicago, that toddlin' town* . . ." and that was when I knew I had forgotten the rest of the words.

Then I saw it coming down the Pike, just a glimpse of metallic blue, a blur with yellow fog-lights that passed in the dusk, and the driver's face was Chester's. I wheeled the bug around, headed back into town, wound the gears tight to gain some speed, but he was too far gone to catch up with. I cruised town for an hour before I saw him barreling down the Pike again, and this time I saw the blond in his car. When they pulled in on Front Street to get a bite at the café, I wheeled up beside the new Camaro. I had seen that girl of his lick her teeth in toothpaste ads on TV.

I asked Chester how it was going, but he forgot to know me: "Beg pardon?" I saw all his teeth were capped, but I told him who I was. "Oh, yes," he said. I asked him where he got the mean machine, and his girl looked at me funny, smiled to herself. "It's a rental." His girl broke out laughing, but I didn't get the joke. I told Chester he ought to go by and say hello to Pop on the way out. "Yes, yes, well, I will." I invited them out to eat with me and my old man, but Chester got a case of rabbit. "Perhaps another time. Nice to see you again." He slammed the car door, went into the café ahead of his girl.

I sat there in the VW, stared at the grease on my jeans, thought I ought to go in there and shove a couple of perhaps-another-times down Chester's shit-sucking face. Don't ask me why I didn't do it, because it was what I wanted most to do all my life, and don't ask me where the dream went, because it never hummed to me again.

When Chester left town, he left a germ. Not the kind of germ you think makes a plant grow, but a disease, a virus, a contagion. Chester sowed them in the café when Deputy recognized him, asked what he'd been doing with himself. Chester told Deputy he was on Broadway, and gave away free tickets to the show he was in, and a whole slough of people went up to New York. They all came back humming show songs. And the germ spread all over Rock Camp, made any kid on the high-school stage think he could be Chester. A couple of the first ones killed themselves, then the real hell was watching the ones who came back, when Pop told them there was no work at the station for faggots.

But one thing was for sure good to know, and that was when Chester was chewed up and spit out by New York because he thought his shit didn't stink, or at least that was what the folks said. I don't know what happened in New York, but I think I've got a hitch on what Chester did here. He was out to kill everybody's magic and make his own magic the only kind, and it worked on those who believed in Archie's heyday, or those who thought the sweet tit would never go dry, and it worked on Chester when he came back, started to believe it himself.

Standing in the station on a slow day, I sometimes think up things that might have happened to Chester, make up little plays for him to act out, wherever he is. When I do that, I very often lose track of when and where I am, and sometimes Pop has to yell at me to put gas in a car because I haven't heard the bell ring. Every time that sort of thing happens, I cross myself with my left hand and go out whistling a chorus of "Chicago."

Check the oil? Yessir.

∗

IN THE DRY

E sees the bridge coming, sees the hurt in it, and says aloud
his name, says, "Ottie." It is what he has been called, and
he says again, "Ottie." Passing the abutment, he glances up, and
in the side mirror sees his face, battered, dirty; hears Bus's voice
from a far-off time, *I'm going to show you something.* He breathes long
and tired, seems to puff out the years since Bus's Chevy slammed
that bridge, rolled, and Ottie crawled out. But somebody told it
that way — he only recalls the hard heat of asphalt where he lay
down. And sometimes, Ottie knows. Now and again, his nerves
bang one another until he sees a fist, a fist gripping and twisting
at once; then hot water runs down the back of his throat, he heaves.
After comes the long wait — not a day or night, but both folding
on each other until it is all just a time, a wait. Then there is no
more memory, only years on the hustle with a semi truck — years
roaring with pistons, rattling with roads, waiting to sift out one
day. For this one day, he comes back.

This hill-country valley is not his place: it belongs to Sheila, to
her parents, to her cousin Buster. Ottie first came from outside
the valley, from the welfare house at Pruntytown; and the Gerlocks raised him here a foster child, sent him out when the money
crop of welfare was spent. He sees their droughty valley, but
cannot understand — the hills to either side can call down rain.

147

Jolting along the Pike, he looks at withered fields, corn tassling out at three feet, the high places worse with yellowish leaves. August seems early for the hills to rust with dying trees, early for embankments to show patches of pale clay between milkweed and thistle. All is ripe for fire.

At a wide berm near the farmhouse, he edges his tractor truck over, and the ignition bell rings out until the engine sputters, dies. He picks up his grip, swings out on the ladder, and steps down. Heat burns through his T-shirt under a sky of white sun; a flattened green snake turns light blue against the blacktop.

The front yard's shade is crowded with cars, and yells and giggles drift out to him from the back. A sociable, he knows, the Gerlock whoop-de-doo, but a strangeness stops him. Something is different. In the field beside the yard, a sin crop grows — half an acre of tobacco standing head-high, ready to strip. So George Gerlock's notions have changed and have turned to the bright yellow leaves that bring top dollar. Ottie grins, takes out a Pall Mall, lets the warm smoke settle him, and minces a string of loose burley between his teeth. A clang of horseshoes comes from out back. He weaves his way through all the cars, big eight-grand jobs, and walks up mossy sandstone steps to the door.

Inside smells of ages and of chicken fried in deep fat, and he smiles to think of all his truckstop pie and coffee. In the kitchen, Sheila and her mother work at the stove, but they stop of a sudden. They look at him, and he stands still.

The old woman says, "Law, it's you." Sunken, dim, she totters to him. "Where on earth, where on earth?"

He takes the weak hand she offers and speaks over her shoulder to Sheila. "Milwaukee. Got to get a tank trailer of molasses from the mill. Just stopped by — didn't mean to barge your sociable."

"Aw, stay," Sheila says. She comes to him and kisses his cheek. "I got all your letters and I saved ever one."

He stares at her. She is too skinny, and her face is peeling from sunburn with flecks of brown still sticking to her cheek, and along her stomach and beneath her breasts, lines of sweat stain her blouse. He laughs. "You might of answered a few of them letters."

The old woman jumps between them. "Otto, Buster's awful bad off. He's in a wheelchair with two of them bags in him to catch his business."

Sheila goes to the stove. "Ottie don't need none of that, Mom. He just got here. Let him rest."

Ottie thinks of the abutment, the wear on his face. "It's them steel plates. They don't never get any better with them plates in their heads."

Old Woman Gerlock's eyes rim red. "But hush. Take your old room — go on now — you can table with us."

Sheila smiles up at him, a sideways smile.

Upstairs, he washes and shaves. Combing out his hair, he sees how thin it has gone, how his jaw caves in where teeth are missing. He stares at the knotted purple glow along the curve of his jaw — the wreck-scar — and knows what the Gerlocks will think, wonders why it matters. No breaks are his; no breaks for foster kids, for scab truckers.

He sits on the edge of the bed, the door half open, and hears talk of the *ugly accident* creep from the kitchen up the stairs. Ottie knows Old Gerlock's voice, and thinks back to how the old man screamed for Bus, how his raspy yells were muffled by saws cutting into twisted metal.

As he tries to find the first thing to turn them all this way, the pieces of broken life fall into his mind, and they fall without the days or nights to mend them. He opens a window, walks back to his low table. Those things are still there: dried insects, Sheila's mussel shells from Two-Mile Creek's shoals, arrowheads, a plaster angel. All things he saved.

He picks up the angel, likes its quiet sadness. A time ago, it peeked through flowers when he came to himself in the hospital, and the old woman prayed by his bed while he scratched the bandage-itch. He hears children shouting. When he was a child, he held a beagle puppy, looked into the trunk of a hollow tree: on the soft inner loam was the perfect skeleton of a mouse, but grabbing for it, his hand brought up a mangle of bones and wet wood. He puts the angel on the table, and looking into the yard, he sees no such tree. *Show you something*

In the hot yard, Gerlocks unfold their tables, and their laughter hurts him. They are double-knit flatlanders long spread to cities: a people of name, not past. He has been in their cities, and has jockeyed his semi through their quiet streets seeing their fine houses. But always from the phone book to the street he went, and never to a doorstep. Fancy outside is fancy inside, and he never needs to look   He knows why they come back — a little more fancy.

The sun makes long light-bars on the floor; walking through them, he thinks of the wire grille bolted to his window at Pruntytown, so far from this valley, and he wonders what became of all the boys waiting for homes. From the closet he takes an old white shirt, its shoulders tan with coat-hanger rust, with years. He puts it on, strains to button it across his chest. He wore this same shirt to church back then, sat alone, saw the fancy way Bus and Sheila dressed. This time he knows himself better, stronger, and it is good to wear the shirt.

On the closet shelf is a box of old photographs of distant Gerlock kin, people from a time so far that names have been forgotten. Years ago, wet winters kept him in, and he laid out pictures, made up lives for these people, and made them his kin and history. He felt himself part of each face, each person, and reached into their days for all he could imagine. Now they seem only pictures, and he carries the box downstairs to the porch.

The back porch catches a breeze, and he lets it slip between the buttons of his shirt, sits in the swing, and listens to the first dead water-maple leaves chattering across the hard-packed path. His hand shuffles through old photographs, some cardboard, some tin. They show the brown and gray faces of Gerlock boys; men he almost knew, old men, all dead. The women are dressed in long skirts; only half-pretty women, too soon gone old. He wonders about the colors of their world: flour-sack print dresses, dark wool suits; a bluer sky by day, a blacker night. Now days and nights blur, and the old clothes are barn rags, brown with tractor grease. He puts the box on the floor, watches the Gerlock families.

The families walk the fields to see how neatly generations laid out this farm. Ottie knows the good way it all fits: hill pasture, an orchard with a fenced cemetery, bottoms for money crops. He can see what bad seasons have done to warp barn siding, to sag fences he drew tight, to hide posts with weeds.

Wasps swarm under the porch's eave. Warming in the late sun, they hover, dip, rise again, and their wings fight to cool the air around their nest. Beyond the hills, where the landline ends, he sees the woods creeping back, taking over with burdock, ironweed, and sassafras. A day forgotten comes to him.

On the spring day he spent with Sheila, they caught a green-gold bass, and watched it dangle as the light sprinkled on it.

Sheila said, "I think the belly's the prettiest part."

Ottie grabbed her, laughed. "All that color and you pick the white?"

Sheila giggled and they held each other, fighting for breath, and leaned against the spotted bark of a sycamore. Then the fish flopped from the hook, and slipped into black water. They sat on roots, rested, listened to their breathing. With his fingers laced under her breasts, Ottie felt her blood pumping.

One wasp reels, circles, butts beaded ceiling, and Ottie watches the brown wings flash over bright yellow bands, and knows he can pack his grip, be in Columbus by midnight. He lights another cigarette, wonders if being with Sheila that day has turned them.

The old woman's voice tunnels through the hall to the porch, a soft cry: "It's for disgrace you want Bus here."

"Done nothing like it," the old man yells. "He's a part of us. He's got a right if the murderous devil yonder has got a right."

Hearing Sheila calm them, he breathes out smoke, rubs fingers along the fine stubble near his scar.

Old Gerlock comes out, Sheila and her yellow dog behind him; Ottie stands to shake hands, looks again at the old man's stiff face. He sees eyes straining from hard years, and there are lines and wrinkles set long ago by the generations trying to build a place.

Old Gerlock says, "Otto."

"Good to see you sir." He feels heavy, stupid, and bends to pet Sheila's dog.

"That's a sugar-dog," Old Gerlock says. "Worthless mutt."

Ottie hears Sheila laugh, but deeper than he remembers. Her laugh was high then, and the old woman worried them around the porch, saying, "Please don't, honey. A thing alive can feel." But Sheila held her paper-cone torch to another nest, careful to keep flames and falling wasps from her hand. She balanced on the banister, held the brace, and he saw the curve of a beginning breast crease her shirt. Then he looked to Bus, knew Bus had seen it too. He stops petting Sheila's dog, and straightens.

The old man paws his shoulder. "Otto, you always got a place here, but when Buster comes, you help make him feel at home."

"Yessir." Bus's face comes back to Ottie: a rage gone beyond fear — the thought almost makes him know. "I hadn't figured he'd be here."

"Soon enough. You don't recollect nothing of what happened?"

"Nosir. Just me and Sheila fishing and Bus coming to say he wants me to ride with him and listen for a noise."

"Not even after all these years?"

Sheila hugs the old man with one arm. "Dad, time just makes it go inside. Ottie won't ever know."

Old Gerlock shuffles and pshaws: "I just figured . . ."

The old woman comes out, a dish towel in her hand, and Ottie watches her gasp to keep down sobs. "Otto, don't you take no disgrace at Bus coming here. Wickedness brung him. Pure-T devilment."

The old man looks hard at her, then to Sheila and Ottie, and his face goes gray-blue with blood. "Sheila, take him yonder to see my new dog — only don't be sugaring over her, now, you can't do such to a hunting dog."

Sheila and Ottie go down the steps, take the clay path to the barn. Ottie squints in the coarse sun. Along low slopes of parched hills, fingers of green twist into gullies where water still hides. Looking back, he sees the old man go inside, but the old woman stands alone, with hands over her eyes.

"This is a hell of a game," Sheila says. "They wasn't going to bring Bus. Then Dad hears you're here — up and calls them, says, 'Bring Buster hell or high water.' "

"Don't matter. Just makes me feel tired, sort of."

She takes his hand. "Why'd you never come in before?"

"Never been back this way. Had to get out sooner or later. I don't see what made you stay."

"No place to go but here. You changed, Ottie. You used to be rough as a damn cob, but you're quiet. Moody quiet the way Bus was."

He squints harder. "What about you?"

"Nothing much happens here. Lots happens to you with all your shifting around. Don't that ever bother you?"

He laughs short and low. "You-all pity me my ways, don't you? Only I'm better off — ain't a thing here to change a one of you."

"Ain't nothing to make us any worse off, if that's what you're after."

153

She looks away from him, and her frizzy hair, faded with the long years, hides her face. At sixteen she was nothing to look at, and he has always dreamed her as looking better. Now he sees her an old maid in a little town, and knows her bitterness.

"This is my last haul anyplace," he says, waits until she looks at him. "I'm getting me a regular job with regular guys. I'm blacklisted, so I can't drive union, but I know a place in Chicago that rebuilds rigs . . ."

"You won't stick, Ottie. You don't know what it is to stay in a place, and there ain't any place you'll stick."

He has half hoped, kept the hope just a picture of thought, a thought of sending Sheila the fare and working regular hours. Now he puts it away, seeing too soon how dim it gets.

He looks into the pen. Old Gerlock's dog is a square-headed hound, and Ottie knows to pet her means nothing. She stares at them blankly, beats her tail in the dusty shadow of her house. Blue-green flies hum her, but she does not snap them the way Beagle had. *Got something, something to show*

When they were boys, he and Bus chopped brush along the fence all that day. Toward dusk, with chimney swifts clouding the sky, they cut into the scattered bones of a white-tailed buck — the yellowed ribs still patchy with leathered meat. Bleached antlers clung to the skull.

Bus up and grabbed the skull as Ottie leaned for it. "Lookee, I bet it was killed by Injuns."

Ottie pulled at an antler until Bus let loose, then chucked the skull into thick green woods. "Hell, them's common as sin." He hooked brush again, stood straight only to watch when Beagle scared up a rabbit, set a sight-chase. He saw Bus far behind him, staring into meshed underbrush. The woods were already dark.

Bus was half crying. "I would of made me a collection like yours."

"Beagle jumped another one," Ottie said. He went back to work, heard Bus whipping with his sickle to catch the pace.

Bus said, "I don't like Beagle."

A bottle fly buzzes Ottie's eyes, and he fans it away, watches Sheila's dog sniff the wire-edged pen. The dog tries to jump over, and Sheila catches his collar.

Ottie says, "Boy and a girl."

"Not this one. He's been fixed."

"Yeah, but they still know what to do." He looks at ridges made brown fire by sun, and thinks back to a boy with mouse bones, a hollow tree, a beagle puppy.

A triangle rings up from the backyard, and Ottie goes with Sheila around the barn; but looking up, he sees them wheel Bus into the shade of a catalpa. Sheila gives Ottie a hasty, worrisome glance, and Ottie walks slowly to Bus, tries to see each day of the hidden time, but only sees the way Bus is now. Bus sits crooked to one side, his hands bone-bunches in his lap, head bending. He is pale, limp, and his face is plaster-quiet. Ottie smells a stink, and knows it is from the bags hanging on the chair.

"Here's Ottie," says Bus's mother. She leans over the chair. "You know Ottie."

Bus looks up at her, and his face wrenches tight. He rocks side to side in his chair. "Cig'ret'." In the shadow of the tree, blue veins show through his skin. A tube runs yellow from his crotch, and he lifts it, drains it into its bag.

"Oh, honey, you smoke so much." She looks at Ottie. "His Uncle George wants him to stop, but it's the only thing he gets any pleasure from."

Ottie shrugs.

"Here's Ottie."

Ottie squats, sticks out his hand. "Hey, Bus."

Bus takes the hand, then growls up at his mother. "Cig'ret'."
He shows his teeth.

Ottie gives him a Pall Mall, lights it. A curl of smoke wisps
Bus's eyes, and he blinks once, slowly. Pieces of tobacco cling to
his gray lips, and he spits weakly at them. The woman's bare hand
wipes her boy's chin. Ottie glances from the grass to Bus's face,
but all the days of waiting are not there, only a calm boy-smile.
Ottie scratches at his scar, and his hand smells of Bus's —
the smell of baby powder and bedsore salve.

"Buster, it's Ottie," she says again.

"Otto." On the porch, the old man holds his Bible against his
chest, one finger parting the leaves.

Ottie stands. "Yessir?"

"Get the plow from the toolshed yonder."

On the path to the shed, a strangeness creeps through him: he
remembers walking this way — nights, years ago — and Bus yell-
ing, "I'm going to show you something, Ottie." Bus grinned,
made Beagle dance on his hind legs by holding back the collar. Then
Bus shoved hard with his sickle blade, and Beagle stumbled,
coughing, into a corner. First his bandy legs folded, then he fell
to his side, did not breathe, and his flanks filled, swelled. Ottie
found no blood, only the pink-lipped wound in one dimple of Beagle's chest. Then he carried the dog toward dark hills.

In the hot shed, he gathers himself and finds the plow. With its
handles and traces rotted away, the blade seems something from
an unreal time, and his fingers track warm metal now pitted with
rust. The Gerlocks always tell that this plow was first to break
the bottoms of their valley, and Ottie wonders what it means or if
they just made it up.

Sawdust falls into his eyes and he steps back, looks to the ceiling;
a bumblebee drills the rafters. The joists are spotted where Old
Gerlock has daubed other holes with axle grease. Still, the bee
drills. Ottie dwells on Sheila's laugh, a laugh high and happy at

burning wasps. He remembers the nest in her hand, the fresh smile on her face, and the wasp worms popping from their paper cells under her fingertips.

He carries the single-blade to the porch, puts it on the banister, and brushes at the rusty streaks on his good shirt, smears brownish dust into the threads. He goes to the yard's edge, away. Sheila comes to stand with him, and he feels her eyes on him from the side, feels her fingers pressing inside his forearm.

On the porch, the old man preaches from his Bible, and his voice is a wind and whisper; the words of his god have the forgotten colors of another time. As the gathered families listen, Ottie watches them, their clothes fitting so well, and he knows the old man is the only Bible-beater among them. He hears false power in the preacher's voice, sees outsiders pretending. Old fool, he thinks, new fools are here to take your place.

Old Gerlock shouts to the hills: "For if they do these things in a green tree, what shall be done in the dry?"

Heads bow to the prayer, the unfixed wish, the hope offered up, and every head turns to Bus.

"Godspeed the plow," they say.

A line forms for supper, and Ottie sees the folding table set for Bus, a special table alone, and he knows Bus has no right — nobody has any right. They should all eat alone, all with no past, no life here.

On another table sit foods long forgotten: pinto beans, fried tomatoes, chowchow relish. He is hungry and keeps close behind Sheila, fills his plate, sits with her where he can see Bus. Old Gerlock wanders to their table, rests skinny arms by his plate as he prays to himself. Sheila elbows Ottie, jerks her head toward her father, and her mouth stretches out to a grin. Ottie shrugs, eats, watches Bus's mother strip chicken and spoon it to her boy.

The old man looks up, blends his food. "Is it a good life, the way you live?"

Ottie puts down his fork the way the old woman taught him. "It keeps me busy enough."

"Must help you forget, I figure."

"Yessir. There's mistreatment galore from you I don't recollect."

Sheila takes Ottie's hand. "Stop it, you two."

The old man's lips go pale with a smile. "Just what happened to wreck that car, Otto?"

A dull flash passes over him; a sickness and a pain streaming from his neck down his back. Beyond the old man sits Bus — Bus with eyes of hard sadness. Ottie knows. "We been through that before."

Sheila squeezes his hand. "Goddamn, let it alone."

The old man draws to hit her, and her head turns.

Ottie yells, "Hit *me*."

Old Gerlock drops his hand. "No, you have got your suffering — just like her." He eats, does not look up.

Bus's eyes fix Ottie with a helpless gaze, but his lips skin back in rage. He sits straight in his chair, one hand waving away the spoon of chicken. He moans, "Ot'ie."

Sheila takes Ottie's arm. "C'mon, that's enough."

He shakes her off, walks under the waning shade of the catalpa, and bends over Bus. He draws his face close, and smells the smoked oil of Bus's skin.

Bus cries, shakes his head, "Ot'ie."

He whispers, tries to hiss, "Bus."

"Ot'ie."

With the lumped knuckles of Bus's hand, he saw the far-hidden minutes of racing along the Pike. He saw Bus's face go stiff to fight, saw the sneer before that hand twisted the wheel a full turn and metal scraped and warped against bridge sides. *Show you, you got some* Ottie looks to the hills: in their hollows were outcrops, shallow caves where he hid with leaf-bedding and fire pit, where he waited out the night beside Beagle's cool carcass.

He squats, puts his hand on Bus's shoulder. "Bus?"

Bus blinks, bows his head.

Standing, Ottie sees the families staring, and he goes from the yard into open, brown bottoms. Sheila follows, catches his hand to slow him. He curves uphill to the orchard, stops at its crest. Far below are black splotches of Two-Mile Creek showing between patches of trees, the only green spreading slowly out from the marshy banks.

He remembers standing in that creek with Old Gerlock. He almost knew again the cool sweep against his knees, felt the hand cover his face, then the dipping into a sudden rush. Only that once he prayed; asked to stay, always live here. Sheila's arms go around his waist.

The ground is thick with fruit: some ripe, some rotten, some blown by yellow jackets. Ottie pulls a knotted apple, bites into dry meal. Even the pulp has no taste, and he sees the trees need pruning. He tosses the fruit away. "We used to cut props for the branches."

"Mom worked me all week making apple butter, but it's been a while." She snorts a small laugh, holds the back of her hand to her forehead, mocks: "Oh, dear. What *shall* we do in the dry?"

"Blow away, I guess."

"Yes," she says, pulls on him. "Asses to asses and bust to bust."

Ottie feels too close, lets go, and watches as she picks up something, holds it out to him. It is the pale blue half of a robin's egg left from the spring.

He says, "They throw it out if it don't hatch."

"You told me that before. I thought you saved such stuff."

He thinks of the low table in his room, the arrowheads, the

159

plaster angel. Again he sees the buck-skull sailing, turning through the branches, shattering. His smile falls away. "No, I quit saving stuff."

She crushes the shell in her palm, makes it blue-white paste. "I ain't never been loved."

"Bullshit, Sheila. Buster loved you."

"Bus?" Her hand shades her eyes against the last sun.

"He thought we was making it down at the creek."

She clasps her hands around his neck, smiles again. "I ain't never even had a man, but I wanted both of you. Didn't you ever want to?"

He shakes his head.

She squints, and her hands slip from around his neck; she backs away, turns, hurries toward the house. Watching her go through timothy and trees, he hopes she will not look back, and hopes she will be lost to him in the crowded yard.

He sits against the cemetery's fence, scratches up dead moss with a stick, and feels the back of his shirt ripping on ribbed bars. The sun makes an ivory scar in the sky behind the hills; from the creek, a killdeer cries flying from marshes into the line of sun. A blue-brown light creeps up from the ground, and the leaves make patterns against a shadowy sky.

One by one, he picks up the fallen leaves nearest him, gathers them to himself with the years of hurried life. Feeling the crinkled edges of a scorched leaf, he sees, in the last of light, colors still splotching its skin. Everything is so far away, so buried, and he knows more than any buck-skull turned them all.

He walks the darkening fields alone. Heat lightning flashes, and he hears the slow drone of locusts cooling in the trees. He wonders how many deer have died in all the winter snows, how many mice have become the dirt. Walking the fencerow, Ottie knows Bus owns this farm, and has sealed it off in time where he can live it every day. And Ottie sees them together a last time: a dying dog and two useless children, forever ghosts, they can neither scream nor play; even dead, they fight over bones.

The cars leave the dusky yard, bound for cities and years far into the night. He stands until the farmhouse lights go out, then walks back through the yard, up to the porch.

"You'll be heading out tomorrow?" Old Gerlock sits hidden away in the shadows.

"Yessir."

"Stick around and help to strip tobacco."

Ottie grins. "Cutting knife don't fit my hand."

"Can't you tell the truth about Buster?"

He shrugs, rubs his hand across his face, but smells no salve or powder; only the dust of leaves. "I reckon Bus was trying to . . . I guess it was accidental."

The old man goes to the door, holds it open, then spits over the banister. "God forgive my wore-out soul, but I hope you burn in hell." Old Gerlock goes inside.

Ottie sits in the swing, thinks of the bars on his window at Pruntytown, and laughs. They never needed bars. They had always been safe from him. *Do what in the dry*

His voice is smoky: "Blow away."

Rustling metal leaves of tintypes, he takes a cardboard picture from the shoe box, lights it, sees the photograph crinkle into orange, blue, and purple against the night. He lights another, makes flames eat the long-forgotten faces. *Blow away* The third he wants to hold to the wasp nest, wants to make singed insects fall through colored flames, wants to see worms bubble and the rough edges of their paper nest smolder. It is not his way of doing. He shakes his head, waves out the fire. He stands until the last spark glows, rises, burns out.

"Blow away."

Inside is close, and it sucks the air from him. .The scent of chicken seeps into the walls and already it is becoming the smell of old times. He takes the stairs quietly, sees no light under Old Gerlock's door, but a film clings to his skin the closer he comes to the landing.

Going down the hall to his old room, he passes Sheila's door, looks up. He sees her standing naked in the doorway; gray, waiting. He stops, waiting; he listens to her breathing. Slowly, he moves up his hand, touches her face, and he feels the sweat of her cheek mingle with the dust of his palm. He knows her better, and he knows her way of doing.

He steps into his room, strips off the white rag, and leaves it lying on the bed. He packs his grip with a razor, soap, and comb, all things he brought. Pulling on a clean T-shirt, he zips shut the grip and carries it into the hall. Sheila's door is closed, and Ottie knows what turned them all will spin them forever.

Outside, the yard is empty, dark. He climbs the ladder into his semi's cab and tries to remember a wide spot by the mill, a place to pull over. The ignition bell rings out, and gears — ten through forward — strain to whine into another night, an awful noise.

FIRST DAY OF WINTER

HOLLIS sat by his window all night, staring at his ghost in glass, looking for some way out of the tomb Jake had built for him. Now he could see the first blue blur of morning growing behind bare tree branches, and beyond them the shadows of the farm. The work was done: silos stood full of corn, hay bales rose to the barn's roof, and the slaughter stock had gone to market; it was work done for figures in a bank, for debts, and now corn stubble leaned in the fields among stacks of fodder laced with frost. He could hear his parents shuffling about downstairs for their breakfast; his old mother giggling, her mind half gone from blood too thick in her veins; his father, now blind and coughing. He had told Jake on the phone, they'll live a long time. Jake would not have his parents put away like furniture. Hollis asked Jake to take them into his parsonage at Harpers Ferry; the farm was failing. Jake would not have room: the parsonage was too modest, his family too large.

He went downstairs for coffee. His mother would not bathe, and the warm kitchen smelled of her as she sat eating oatmeal with his father. The lids of the blind man's eyes hung half closed and he had not combed his hair; it stuck out in tufts where he had slept on it.

"Cer'al's hot." His mother giggled, and the crescent of her mouth made a weak grin. "Your daddy's burnt his mouth."

"I ain't hungry." Hollis poured his coffee, leaned against the sink.

The old man turned his head a little toward Hollis, bits of meal stuck to his lips. "You going hunting like I asked?"

Hollis sat his cup in the sink. "Thought I'd work on the car. We can't be with no way to town all winter because you like squirrel meat."

The old man ate his cereal, staring ahead. "Won't be Thanksgiving without wild game."

"Won't be Thanksgiving till Jake and Milly gets here," she said.

"They said last night they ain't coming down," his father said, and the old woman looked at Hollis dumbly.

"I got to work on the car," Hollis said, and went toward the door.

"Car's been setting too long," the old woman yelled. "You be careful of snakes."

Outside, the air was sharp, and when the wind whipped against his face, he gasped. The sky was low, gray, and the few Angus he had kept from market huddled near the feeder beside the barn. He threw them some hay, brought his tool chest from the barn, began to work on the car. He got in to see if it would start, ground it. As he sat behind the wheel, door open, he watched his father come down from the porch with his cane. The engine's grinding echoed through the hollows, across the hills.

Hollis's knuckles were bloody, scraped under the raised hood, and they stung as he turned the key harder, gripped the wheel. His father's cane tapped through the frosty yard, the still of December, and came closer to Hollis. The blind man's mouth was shut against the cold, the dark air so close to his face, and Hollis stopped trying the engine, got out.

"You can tell she's locking up." The blind man faced him.

"This ain't a tractor." Hollis walked around, looked under the hood, saw the hairline crack along one side of the engine block.

His father's cane struck the fender, and he stood still and straight beside his son. Hollis saw his father's fingers creeping along the grille, holding him steady. "She sounded locked up," he said again.

"Yeah." Hollis edged the man aside, shut the hood. He didn't have the tools to pull the engine, and had no engine to replace it.

"Maybe Jake'll loan you the money for a new car."

"No," the old man said. "We'll get by without bothering Jake."

"Put it on the cuff? Do you think the bank would give us another nickel?"

"Jake has too much to worry with as it is."

"I asked him to take you-all last night."

"Why?"

"I asked him and Molly to take you in and he said no. I'm stuck here. I can't make my own way for fighting a losing battle with this damn farm."

"Farming's making your way."

"Hell."

"Everybody's trying for something better anymore. When everybody's going one way, it's time to turn back." He rationalized in five directions.

In the faded morning the land looked scarred. The first snows had already come, melted, and sealed the hills with a heavy frost the sun could not soften. Cold winds had peeled away the last clinging oak leaves, left the hills a quiet gray-brown that sloped into the valley on either side.

He saw the old man's hair bending in the wind.

"Come on inside, you'll catch cold."

"You going hunting like I asked?"

"I'll go hunting."

As he crossed the last pasture heading up toward the ridges, Hollis felt a sinking in his gut, a cold hunger. In the dry grass he shuffled toward the fence line to the rising ridges and high stand of oaks. He stopped at the fence, looked down on the valley and the farm. A little at a time Jake had sloughed everything to him, and now that his brother was away, just for this small moment, Hollis was happier.

He laid down his rifle, crossed the fence, and took it up again. He headed deeper into the oaks, until they began to mingle with the yellow pine along the ridge. He saw no squirrels, but sat on a stump with oaks on all sides, their roots and bottom trunk brushed clean by squirrel tails. He grew numb with waiting, with cold; taking a nickel from his pocket, he raked it against the notched stock, made the sound of a squirrel cutting nuts. Soon enough he saw a flick of tail, the squirrel's body hidden by the tree trunk. He tossed a small rock beyond the tree, sent it stirring and rattling the leaves, watched as the squirrel darted to the broadside trunk. Slowly, he raised his rifle, and when the echoes cleared from the far hills across the valley, the squirrel fell. He field-dressed it, and the blood dried cold on his hands; then he moved up the ridge toward the pine thicket, stopping every five minutes to kill until the killing drained him and his game bag weighed heavily at his side.

He rested against a tree near the thicket, stared into its dark wavings of needles and branches; there, almost blended with the red needles, lay a fox. He watched it without moving, and thought of Jake, hidden, waiting for him to break, to move. In a fit of meanness, he snapped his rifle to his shoulder and fired. When he looked again the fox was gone, and he caught a glimpse of its white-tipped tail drifting through the piny darkness.

Hollis dropped the gun, sat against the tree, and, when the wind snatched at his throat, fumbled to button his collar. He felt old and tired, worn and beaten, and he thought of what Jake had said about the state home he wanted the folks in. They starve them, he said, and they mistreat them, and in the end they smother them.

For a moment, Hollis wondered what it would be like to smother them, and in the same moment caught himself, laughing; but a darkness had covered him, and he pulled his gloves on to hide the blood on his hands. He stumbled up, and, grabbing his gun, ran between trees to the clearing nearest the fence, and when he crossed into the pasture felt again a light mist of sweat on his face, a calming.

He crossed the fields and fences, slogged across the bottoms and up to the house. Inside, his mother sat in the tiny back room, listening, with the husband, to quiet music on the radio. She came to Hollis, and he saw in her wide-set eyes a fear and knowledge — and he knew she could see what insanity had driven him to.

He handed her the squirrels, dressed and skinned, from his game bag, and went to wash his hands. From the corner of his eye, he saw her, saw as she dropped the squirrels into soaking brine, saw her hand go up to her mouth, saw her lick a trace of blood and smile.

Sitting at the table, he looked down at his empty plate, waited for the grace, and when it was said, passed the plate of squirrel. He had taken for himself only the forequarters and liver, leaving the meaty hinds and saddles.

"Letter come from Jake." The ol man held a hindquarter, gnawed at it.

"And pitchers of them." His mother got up, came back with a handful of snapshots.

"He done fine for himself. Lookee at the pretty church and the children," she said.

The church was yellow brick and low, stained windows. In the picture Jake stood holding a baby, his baby girl, named after their mother. His face was squinted with a smile. The old woman poked

167

a withered finger into the picture. "That's my Mae Ellen," she said. "That's my favorite."

"Shouldn't have favorites." His father laid down the bones.

"Well, you got to face that he done fine for himself."

Hollis looked out the window; the taste of liver, a taste like acorns, coated his mouth with cold grease. "Coming snow," he said.

His father laughed. "Can't feel it."

"Jake says they're putting a little away now. Says the church is right nice people."

"They ain't putting away enough to hear him tell it."

"Now," she said, "he's done fine, just let it be."

When the meal was finished, Hollis pushed back his chair. "I asked Jake to help by taking you-all in; he said no."

The old man turned away; Hollis saw tears in his blind eyes, and that his body shook from crying. He wagged his head again and again. The old woman scowled, and she took up the plates, carried them to the sink. When she came back, she bent over Hollis.

"What'd you figure he'd say? He's worked like an ox and done good, but he can't put us all up."

The old man was still crying, and she went to him, helped him from the chair. He was bent with age, with crying, and he raised himself slowly, strung his flabby arm around the woman's waist. He turned to Hollis. "How could you do such a goddamned thing as that?"

"We'll take our nap," she said. "We need our rest."

Hollis went to the yard, to where his car stood, looked again at the cracked block. He ran his hand along the grille where the old man's hands had cleared away dust. The wind took his breath, beat on him, and the first light flecks of ice bounced from the fenders. The land lay brittle, open, and dead.

He went back to the house, and in the living room stretched out on the couch. Pulling the folded quilt to his chest, he held it there like a pillow against himself. He heard the cattle lowing to be fed, heard the soft rasp of his father's crying breath, heard his mother's broken humming of a hymn. He lay that way in the graying light and slept.

The sun was blackened with snow, and the valley closed in quietly with humming, quietly as an hour of prayer.

AFTERWORD

I FIRST met Breece Pancake in the spring of 1975, a little more than four years before he killed himself. He was big, raw-boned, slightly slope-shouldered. He looked like one who'd done some hard work outdoors. At that time he had a job teaching English at the Fork Union Military Academy. He put the student-cadets to bed at ten and then wrote from taps till past midnight. He got up with the boys at the six-o'clock reveille. Breece showed up in my office at the University of Virginia one day and asked me to look at some things he'd written. The first story I read was pretty good; it turned out to be the best of his old stuff. Possibly he was testing me with something old before showing the pieces he'd just done. He asked me to look at some more, and luckily I said yes. The next batch were wonderful.

At that time the University of Virginia didn't have much money for writing-students, so I tried to send Breece off to Iowa for a year to get him some more time to write. Iowa wanted him, but they were running low on funds. Breece got a job at the Staunton Military Academy for the next year and started coming to my story-writing class at the university. I thought he should start sending his stories out, but he held back for a while.

Breece had gone to college at Marshall University in Huntington, West Virginia, but what was striking about his knowledge and his craft was how much he'd taken in on his own. He must have had an enormous concentration at an early age. He had a very powerful *sense* of things. Almost all his stories are set in the part of West Virginia that he came from, and he knew that from top to bottom. He knew people's jobs, from the tools they used to how they felt about them. He knew the geology, the prehistory, and the history of his territory, not as a pastime but as such a deep part of himself that he couldn't help dreaming of it. One of the virtues of his writing is the powerful, careful gearing of the physical to the felt.

He worked as hard at his writing as anyone I've known, or known about. I've seen the pages of notes, the sketches, the numbers of drafts, the fierce marginal notes to himself to expand this, to contract that. And of course the final versions, as hard and brilliantly worn as train rails.

When he sold his first story to *The Atlantic* he scarcely took a breath. (He did do one thing by way of celebration. The galley proofs came back with the middle initials of his name set up oddly: Breece *D'J* Pancake. He said fine, let it stay that way. It made him laugh, and, I think, it eased his sense of strain — the strain of trying to get things perfect — to adopt an oddity committed by a fancy magazine.) He was glad, but the rhythm of his work didn't let him glory or even bask. He had expected a great deal from his work, and I think he began to feel its power, but he also felt he was still far from what he wanted.

Not long before Breece and I got to be friends, his father and his best friend both died. Sometime after that Breece decided to become a Roman Catholic and began taking instruction. I'm as uncertain finally about his conversion as I am about his suicide. I've thought about both a lot, and I can imagine a lot, but there is nothing certain I would dare say. Except that it was (and still is) startling to have had that much fierce passion so near, sometimes so close.

Breece asked me to be his godfather. I told him I was a weak reed, but that I would be honored. This godfather arrangement soon turned upside down. Breece started getting after me about going to mass, going to confession, instructing my daughters. It wasn't so much out of righteousness as out of gratitude and affection, but he could be blistering. And then penitent.

As with his other knowledge and art, he took in his faith with intensity, almost as if he had a different, deeper measure of time. He was soon an older Catholic than I was. I began to feel that not only did he learn things fast, absorb them fast, but he aged them fast. His sense of things fed not only on his own life but on others' lives too. He had an authentic sense, even memory, of ways of being he couldn't have known firsthand. It seemed he'd taken in an older generation's experience along with (not in place of) his own.

He was about to turn twenty-seven when he died; I was forty. But half the time he treated me (and I treated him) as if I were his kid brother. The other half of the time he treated me like a senior officer in some ancient army of his imagination. I knew a few things, had some rank, but he felt surely that I needed some looking after. There was more to it than that of course. More than these cartoon panels can show, he was a powerful, restless friend.

After his year commuting from Staunton, we got some money for him. The creative-writing program at the university was co-incidentally, and luckily, endowed, and Breece was among the first to get one of the new fellowships. He had time now to get to know some of the other writers on the faculty (Peter Taylor, James Alan McPherson, Richard Jones) and some of the new band of graduate students in writing. This was on the whole, good. The University of Virginia English department is a sophisticated place, both in a good, wide sense and a bad, narrow sense. The program in writing is just one of the many subdivisions — which is also, on the whole, good. On the good side, there were (and are) people on the regular faculty and among the regular Ph.D. candidates who understood and cared for Breece and his work. On the bad side of life in the department, there is a neurotic cancellation of direct, open expression, perhaps out of self-consciousness about how one's opinion will be regarded, since opinion is the chief commodity. Sometimes it's hard to get a straight answer. And sometimes it's clear that some people hold that criticism is the highest bloom of the literary garden, and that actual stories or novels or poems are the compost.

There was just enough of this attitude to give a young writer, however good, a sense of what social theorists call "status-degradation." Breece didn't know how good he was; he didn't know how much he knew; he didn't know that he was a swan instead of an ugly duckling. This difficulty subsided for Breece, but there was always some outsider bleakness to his daily life, a feeling that he was at the university on sufferance.

Of course, Breece could be pretty thorny himself, and he spent some time getting mad uselessly — that is, over things that I thought were better ignored, or at the wrong people. One effect of Breece's irritated energy was that he began campaigning for an M.F.A. degree for the apprentice writers, a so-called "terminal degree" to replace the uneasy M.A. The university now offers an M.F.A. in English, and it's on the whole an improvement in that it's a license for some of the subsistence-level jobs a writer might need along the way. Breece was a good union man.

He was also a wonderful reader. He screened prose fiction submissions for *Virginia Quarterly Review* and, in the spring of 1979, for the Hoyns Fellowships. He and I and another friend of ours went through a bale (that's a file-cabinet drawer, stuffed). In some ways we were engaged in the most functional form of criticism — picking twelve potential writers out of the bale.

From his clearheadedness and good humor then, and from the way his work was going, I guessed Breece was in good shape. He'd sold another two stories. He gave a reading of yet another to a full house. He had some job prospects, and he was getting ready to leave Charlottesville. He began giving away his possessions to his friends. He'd always been a generous gift-giver — when he came for a meal he'd bring trout he caught, or something for my daughters (for example, bathtub boats he'd whittled, with rubber-band-powered paddle wheels). When he began to give away his things, it looked as if he was just preparing to travel light.

A month later a friend of his showed me a letter from Breece in which he'd written, "If I weren't a good Catholic, I'd consider getting a divorce from life."

No one close to him guessed. Even that sentence about getting a divorce from life is only clear in retrospect. And from other signs and letters it's hard to say how intentional, how accidental his state of mind was when he killed himself.

Breece had a dream about hunting that he logged in his notebooks, I think not long before he died. In the dream there were wooded mountains and grassy bottomland. Clear streams. Game was abundant. But best of all, when you shot a quail, a rabbit, or a deer, it fell dead and then popped back to life and darted off again.

There are a number of things that strike me about this dream. One is that it's about immortality and paradise. It is the happy hunting ground. And so it's still another case of a lore that Breece acquired sympathetically and folded into his own psyche. But the most powerful element is this: a theme of Breece's life and stories is the bending of violence into gentleness. He struggled hotly to be a gentle person.

One of Breece's favorite quotations was from the Bible — Revelation 3:15–16.

> I know thy works, that thou art neither cold nor hot: I would thou wert cold or hot.
> So then because thou art lukewarm, and neither cold nor hot, I will spew thee out of my mouth.

This is a dangerous pair of verses. Untempered by other messages, by the gentler tones of voice of the Spirit, they can be a scourge. It may have been simply a bad accident that Breece didn't allow himself the balms that were available to him after his self-scourgings.

I have three kinds of reminders of Breece. The first is the surprising number of people who have come by to talk about their friendships with him, or who have sent me copies of their correspondence with him. They all know how bristly Breece could be, how hard on himself. (On one postcard to a friend, in the spot for the return address, which was 1 Blue Ridge Lane, Breece wrote: "One Blow Out Your Brain." The friend hadn't noticed it. But the *message* on the card was to encourage the friend — keep on, keep on writing, have a good time, damn it.) But these people speak more of what Breece gave them by his heat.

I also have what Breece wrote.

And then there is a third way — perhaps memory, perhaps a ghost. I'm not sure what ghosts are. The reflective, skeptical answer I give myself is that the vivid sense of dead people that you sometimes have may be like the phantom-limb syndrome — you still feel the arm that's been cut off, still touch with the missing fingers. In like manner, you feel the missing person.

Two weeks after Breece's death, and after a lot of people who knew Breece peripherally had asked the inevitable unanswerable question, I was walking home, dog-tired. It was about two A.M. I was on the Lawn, going toward the Rotunda, the dome bright under the moon. I was walking automatically and only slowly realized I'd stopped. I smelled something. I tasted metal in my mouth. I didn't recognize the smell for an instant. It was a smell I'd known well years before. Gun bluing. But inside this sense of taste and smell was a compelling sympathy, beyond the sympathy of *that's* what it smelled like to have the muzzle in his mouth. There was a deep, terrifying thrill that I would never have dreamed of, a thrill and a temptation that sucked at the whole body. I wouldn't have thought of that. I wouldn't have *dared* to think of that.

In that dizzy urgency of sense, even while I was opening to it, there was something reassuring about it. As much as the letter he left, it was alarming, but loving: Don't go on thinking about why. Feel what I felt for an instant.

Breece and I used to argue a lot. The rhythm of it would often be that he would get up and go just before he lost his temper. He'd come back into my office after a bit and either tell me calmly I was still wrong, or say something funny, allowing he might be not *entirely* right. Now that my own temper's worse, I appreciate his efforts. A month after the experience on the lawn, I was lying in the bathtub trying to think of nothing. I heard a short laugh. Then Breece's voice, an unmistakable clear twang: "That's one way to get the last word."

You don't have to believe anything but this — that's just the way he said things.

There were several more of these sentences over the next year. One a rebuke, the next two gently agreeable. Then recently, again late at night in a lukewarm bath, only a distant murmuring. What? I thought. What?

"— It's all right. You've got your own conscience."

Now there's the less excited working of my mind alone: Breece would have liked this or that, this stream, this book, this person.

This would have made him angry, this made him laugh. A lot of people miss him, and miss what he would have gone on to write.

I think about the many things I learned from Breece. I think, with somewhat more certainty than a wish, that Breece's troubles don't trouble him or the people who struggled with him and loved him, that a good part of what he earned from struggling with his troubles remains.

JOHN CASEY